Acclaim for Gustaw Herling and *The Island*

"A revelation. . . . Gustaw Herl[ing] . . . [one of the most] *thinkers* writing fiction today."

  —Mark Lilla, Contributing E[ditor]

"The weight of his Eastern European experience, the depths to which he descends while meditating on human nature, the stunning ease with which his imagination makes past epochs alive, the incomparable knack for storytelling—all that combined makes one wonder time and again why Gustaw Herling has not yet been recognized in the West as what he so self-evidently is; one of the century's masters."

  —Stanislaw Baranczak, author of *Breathing Under Water and Other Eastern European Essays*

"Like Conrad before him, Gustaw Herling possesses an exceptional—almost uncanny—ability to evoke the essence of cultures alien to his own. . . . [His] penetration of the Italian peasant ethos carries complete conviction, and his identification with that society has all the appearance of native authority."

  —Marese Murphy, *The Irish Times*

"A marvelous story-teller, Herling's [novellas] have the flavour of legend . . . the prose is measured and beautifully, artfully constructed . . . [Herling] is a master craftsman, splendidly in control of his material."

  —Kathy O'Shaughnessy, *Observer*

"Herling is a genius, and by now the most famous Polish writer . . . . He combines a sort of brilliant razor sharpness with a solidity and probing fingers. . . . Here is a writer as passionate and as terrible, as terribly convincing as any now writing . . . the pain in Herling's writings is present only as it is in certain Italian masters of painting. . . . This volume is astonishing. . . . Gustaw Herling is one of the greatest European writers."

  —Peter Levi, *The Independent*

PENGUIN BOOKS

THE ISLAND

Gustaw Herling was born near Kielce, Poland, in 1919. In 1939 he helped to found an anti-Nazi underground organization in Warsaw. Following his arrest in the Russian-occupied sector of Poland in 1940, he spent two years in a Soviet slave labor camp on the White Sea. His experiences there are described in his acclaimed memoir *A World Apart*. After his release by the Russians, Herling joined the Polish army. He is a long-time contributor to *Kultura*, a review published by the celebrated émigré publishing house Instytut Literacki. After the Second World War, Herling eventually settled in Naples, Italy, where he still lives.

THE ISLAND

THREE TALES

GUSTAW HERLING

Translated by Ronald Strom

PENGUIN BOOKS

PENGUIN BOOKS

Published by the Penguin Group

Penguin Books USA Inc., 375 Hudson Street,
New York, New York 10014, U.S.A.
Penguin Books Ltd, 27 Wrights Lane, London W8 5TZ, England
Penguin Books Australia Ltd, Ringwood, Victoria, Australia
Penguin Books Canada Ltd, 10 Alcorn Avenue,
Toronto, Ontario, Canada M4V 3B2
Penguin Books (N.Z.) Ltd, 182–190 Wairau Road,
Auckland 10, New Zealand

Penguin Books Ltd, Registered Offices: Harmondsworth, Middlesex, England

First published in the United States of America by World Publishing 1967
Published by Viking Penguin, a division of Penguin Books USA Inc., 1993
Published in Penguin Books 1994

1 3 5 7 9 10 8 6 4 2

"The Island" and "The Tower" were originally published in Polish by
the Institut Littéraire, Paris, © 1960, under the title *Skrzydia Oltarza*.
"The Second Coming" was originally published by the Institut
Littéraire, © 1963, under the title *Drugie Przyschiez*.

THE LIBRARY OF CONGRESS HAS CATALOGUED THE HARDCOVER AS FOLLOWS:
Herling-Grudzinski, Gustaw, 1919–
[Selections. English. 1993]
The island: three tales/Gustaw Herling; translated by Ronald Strom.
p. cm.
Contents: The island—The tower—The second coming.
ISBN 0-670-84002-5 (hc.)
ISBN 0 14 02.3279 6 (pbk.)
1. Herling-Grudzinski, Gustaw, 1919– —Translations into English. I. Strom,
Ronald. II. Title.
PG7158.H446A27 1993
891.8′537—dc20   92–31452

Printed in the United States of America

CONTENTS

THE ISLAND

We are forsaken like children lost in
the woods. When you stand before me
and look at me, what do you know of
my sufferings and what do I know of
yours? And if I fell at your feet and
cried and told you, would you know
any more about me than you know
about hell when they say it is hot and
sets one shivering? Therefore we men
should stand before each other with as
much awe, thoughtfulness, and love as
before the gates of hell.

FRANZ KAFKA
From a letter to Oscar Pollak (1903)

I

Although it was the middle of May 1950,
there still were not many tourists. Once a day when
the boat came from Naples, the funicular, like a trawl,
would haul a group of people up from the harbor below
and unload them in the square. They would stop for a
moment among the tables of the only café, take a quick
glance around at the people, look up at the clock tower
as if they wanted to remember the precise hour of their
arrival, and then disappear down the narrow streets
and paths into the depths of the island.

The weather was sunny and cool. Between late afternoon and dusk, as the sun withdrew behind the cover of Monte del Sole, the people around the tables of the café slowly emerged from the shadow of their reveries and looked around the square for the still-warm patches of sunset luster. In the morning some of the tourists from the northern countries went down to the sea, but even they returned to the town right after their swim and waited patiently, not hurrying the season.

Spring came late that year. It had been hot, almost scorching, in January and February, and then the winter rains fell. In March and April the sky hid behind low clouds, the air turned sooty like the glass of a kerosene lamp, and a fire burned on the hearth of more than one house on the island. The sea, the color of bluing in dirty soapsuds, pounded monotonously against the rocky shore. Occasionally the hazy outlines of the mainland and the neighboring islands were visible.

At the beginning of May a clear dry wind brought the island's overdue spring. The sea calmed; lightly wrinkled in the morning, splashed with sun at noon, it seemed to paste translucent flakes of blue-green along the shore. The vegetation of gardens and vineyards, of pine woods and fruit trees glowed against the tawny yellow background of rocky cliffs and naked mountain ridges. All the magic of the water, the stone, and the secret filters of the sky oozing in from the outside came to life again in the island's grottoes—the Green Grotto, the Azure Grotto, the Violet Grotto. And the church bells chimed as if they were alloyed of glass and metal.

The island is a three-hour boat ride from Naples, and has no tourist sights other than the paltry ruins of a few Roman villas and the Certosa, a medieval Carthusian monastery. But tourists do not bring history texts or guide books with them to the island. For the tourists the island is, above all, "the pearl of the Mediterranean" of the travel posters, where the sea is clearer and more beautiful than anywhere else in the bay of Naples; where the summer sun toasts the skin for ten hours a day; where the rose wine quickens the blood; where the little houses are plastered white, their brightly colored shutters standing out boldly in the glittering light; where wooden sandals click pleasantly along the pavement; where a little rowboat carries one into a kingdom of silver shadows in the underground grottoes; where songs are full of tender words; where the lights of Naples glitter on the far horizon and the *lampare* of fishing boats twinkle around the island on sultry lazy nights; and where the stars quiver like cooling cinders around the full moon, red as the heart of a volcano. When there is nothing to do in the two hours between sunset and nightfall, the tourists sometimes climb up to the remains of the Roman past, a vantage point from which they have the most extensive view of the island and the bay; or they circle the Certosa in a lazy stroll on the only plateau of any size between the sea and the town.

It is different for the inhabitants of the island. Making their living primarily from tourism, they have adapted the rhythm of their lives, rather than to farming or fishing, to the trawl that during the season hauls tourists up by the hundreds from the harbor to the square. Besides, the soil is barren. Here and there, after removing the surface layer of building stone, the islanders have made the land support small vineyards, little fields, vegetable gardens, olive trees, and lemon and orange; the nets cast out near the shore sparkle grudgingly with the scanty catch. And that is why not only the two hours between sunset and nightfall but all the long months after the end of the season are empty for the inhabitants. Then they live alone with their island.

In their minds its history does not really reach back as far as the time when the sovereigns and patricians of Rome built their villas on the two extremities of the island, known today as Monte della Madonna dei Marini and Monte del Faro. If the inhabitants like to visit these places it is not merely for the remains of ancient walls dug up by archeologists, or for the fragments of friezes, armless statues, and marble baths lying in the grass; they also like to look at the tall slender Madonna who stands on the brink of the precipice facing the sea and watches over seafarers with her arms raised against storm and gale, and near her, the tiny church where in the summer Padre Rocca says mass in the presence of scarcely a single person; and on the other end of the island the lighthouse, which, with its reflectors, performs in a different way the same function as the Madonna of Seafarers with her outstretched arms and her sweet eyes.

More vivid in the minds and feelings of the inhabitants of the island is the medieval Certosa. Every year on the nineteenth of September the large, polychrome wood sculpture of the *Pietà dell'Isola*—the Mother holding in her drooping arms the Son taken from the Cross—emerges from the Certosa in a litter borne on the shoulders of four *Certosini*. Beyond the gate the waiting crowd joins the four monks and, amid the flowers and paper streamers thrown by children dressed in white, to the chanting and ringing of bells, the procession moves along slowly in time to the strained step of the monks down to the main church in the square. At night the whole square is illuminated with colored lamps. The day the *Pietà dell'Isola* makes the trip down to the main church and back is the island's greatest holiday and at the same time the culmination of the season. Soon after, the tourists begin to leave the island and many of them, particularly those from the northern countries, carry away with them like a parting souvenir of their vacation the memory of that strange *festa*, unable either to understand or accept the contrast between the gay humor of the faithful and the symbol of suffering and pain borne with such difficulty by the four monks.

The history of the Certosa and of this ceremony, however, is worth closer examination.

II

The Certosa was founded in the fourteenth century. A representative of the most powerful family on the island, a man who served as secretary to Joan I of Anjou in nearby Naples, built it at his own expense to celebrate the birth of his first son. He endowed it with land, money, papal bulls, religious prerogatives, and numerous privileges to ensure for all time its temporal and spiritual inheritance.

The site could not have been better selected. In accordance with the monastic rule and with a view to preserving the spirit, the monks in their cells could not see beyond the arched line of the shore and a hardly perceptible strip of sea beyond it on the horizon; on the sides, two hills overgrown with pine and olive cut them off from the world. In accordance, too, with the rule of pirate warfare and with a view to preserving the flesh, the low and rather hidden location of the Certosa screened it from observation and from the weapons of the Saracens.

But it did not reward its founder with the good

fortune he expected. After the dethronement and murder of Joan of Anjou, he was banished, his possessions were confiscated, and only by an act of exceptional grace was he permitted to await his death as a penitent and pilgrim behind the same walls he had had erected years before out of gratitude for his firstborn and to the greater glory of Heaven among his descendants. Having ransomed his son from captivity, the monks gave their indirect benefactor, as well, refuge in the Certosa.

Thus, as the founder of the Certosa had formerly repaid Providence for his short-lived good fortune on this earth, so the Certosa settled accounts with him later, when wise Providence neglected his wordly affairs in order to press him, along with his son, into the service of that power and glory which are more enduring than that which he had hitherto served. It led him onto the road of happiness—not the road that glows with worldly splendor and immediate reward, but the road that is more genuine and less ephemeral.

If one can believe the chroniclers who were his contemporaries, the founder of the Certosa, once he had exchanged his princely mantle for the penitent's habit, understood this lesson better than his protectors and hosts; he was the only great and sincere penitent behind the wall. The wealth of the Certosa, considerable even at the time of its founding, grew continuously, and it did not remain without influence—fatal in the opinion of the chronicles—on the life of several monks. Surrounded by servants, excited by their ever-increasing earnings from the cultivated land (particularly the vineyards), they gradually forgot the object of their cloistered isolation from the world and in the end became the gentlemen landlords of the island. The monks squeezed it like a cluster of grapes in the press of taxes and leases and only rarely came to the aid of the needy. Again the hand of God intervened, but almost two centuries had to pass before that happened. In spite of its apparently safe and secure location, the Certosa was burned and completely plundered by Dragut the corsair in the middle of the sixteenth century. It took ten years to rebuild it, and this time a tower was added, from which at last one could see the whole seashore. The Certosa returned to its former affluence after the plague of 1656, having received the inheritance of all those island families who died out without heirs. Again there began a period of material prosperity, fatal to all hermits, together with the sometimes open warfare that the poor clergy of of the island waged against the monks. Thus when Joseph Bonaparte abolished the monasteries and confiscated their possessions in 1807, no one on the island (with the probable exception of the monks themselves) shed tears over the condemned Certosa. The sentence was not revoked, even upon the restoration of the Bourbons. An unusual sign of Providence marked the end of the Certosa's splendor: when the Certosini abandoned the island in 1808, the tower, which had been built in the sixteenth century to defend them from the pirates, collapsed. This reminded the island chroniclers that, a few days before the death of the Roman emperor in the villa on what is now Monte della Madonna dei Marini, another tower had collapsed—a signal tower in the place where today the Madonna watches over seafarers.

The island's aversion for the Certosa was not, however, fed exclusively by the monks' greed and material egotism; it went deeper, to the events of 1656, which revealed other aspects of their egotism a hundred times more incompatible with the calling of knights of the legions of God.

The plague had been reaping an abundant harvest in Naples for some months. Abandoned corpses lay scattered under the walls of buildings in the streets and alleys; the burial carts came for them ever less frequently; the people passed by at a distance; the churches were deserted; a funeral lament mingled in the air with the black smoke of burning beds, straw mattresses, and clothes of those who had died from the pestilence. The black columns of smoke, floating freely in the windless, limpid Neapolitan sky often assumed ominous shapes, neither altogether human nor altogether bestial. Perhaps it was only these columns of smoke that kept the inhabitants of the island, as they looked out at the vault of the bay, from forgetting the scourge that was mercilessly lashing the city on the mainland. Although the smoke brought the news of the plague, fortunately, it was unable to bring the plague itself. The island lived in continual alarm, but the passing days, sluggish like those funeral banners of a smoky shroud, slowly strengthened the conviction that one could, after all, trust in the buckler of the sea, although how flimsy and weak it had been against enemy attacks! One may well imagine that in spite of the islanders' age-old intimacy with the sea, in spite of the many good turns for which they had been indebted to it in the past, only then did the habitants of the island really come to love it.

But the sea did not withstand the assault of the plague. The sea failed the islanders and cracked at the beginning of June. There are two contradictory accounts of the stratagem the pestilence used to breach the island's sea armor and to penetrate the camp of the besieged. In both accounts, however, the figure of the betrothed—the immortal Italian *promesso sposo*—plays the leading role. According to one version the betrothed stole to the island from Naples in order to examine at first hand the dowry of his bride-to-be, and along with his own bacillus of avarice he dragged with him the Neapolitan bacillus of the plague. The other betrothed was the hero of a much more romantic story. Even before the outbreak of the plague he had been banished from Naples to the island for his part in the popular revolt led by Masaniello against the Spaniards, and during the period of the pestilence the young man received from the family of his beloved, who had died in Naples, a letter with a lock of her hair. Beside its romanticism, which appeals more immediately to the imagination, this version seems more in keeping with the nature of plagues and cataclysms—in which the fate of thousands of people always hangs by a thread.

June 1. Three days before the appearance of the plague the census of the island, still preserved in the local archives, mentioned the figure of 1,588 inhabitants. By November 1, when no incident of death or illness had been noted for a week and the epidemic was considered extinguished, the island's revised sad census counted 1,023 inhabitants. The greatest mortality occurred in the scorching month of August, which entered 137 victims in the archival registers.

On June 4, at the news of the arrival of the plague, eighteen monks locked the gate of the Certosa and cut themselves off from the world, creating an island sheltered by thick walls within the island. The inhabitants of the island were stunned with horror: if the cloistered rule of isolation and turning one's back on earthly matters was sometimes more a flight from the Cross than its acceptance, it was certainly so in that time of calamity. It was not only a matter of the resources of the Certosa, although in view of the gradually paralyzed agriculture and fishing on the island, that too must have had its weight. It was also, and perhaps that above all, a matter of human solidarity in suffering, peril, and death. Nothing so exasperates human hearts as the sight of shoulders that refuse to bear the common fate. At best, Naples could look on the island, still untouched by the pestilence, with bitterness and envy; with the tightening of the ring of misfortune, the island must have looked at its *own* island beyond the walls of the Certosa with altogether unbridled hatred.

At the beginning, the island revealed its hatred in oblique glances at that immense mass of gray stone, like an impregnable fortified castle, silent in its detached contempt for the surrounding pestilence. But in July enraged despair drove the island to a more glaring demonstration of feelings hitherto forcibly repressed. The chronicles report that after sunset on July 13, unidentified persons threw the corpses of two of the plague-stricken over the wall into the Certosa. This newly discovered practice continued in a sporadic and covert manner until the end of the month. In August, when the number of deaths suddenly increased, the attack of corpses was intensified and no longer took place under cover of night, but openly in the full blaze of the *solleone*, the most violent sun of the south. From the *Chiostro Grande* the handful of monks, surrounded by death, moved to the *Chiostro Piccolo*. In vain. The column of dead besiegers reached them there too, by way of a narrow path between the side wall and the steep slope of one of the hills.

The retreating monks had one remaining bastion that

was relatively protected, the *Giardino del Priore*, the Prior's Garden, on the edge of an escarpment that fell steeply down to the sea and was inaccessible from without. But who could be sure that the plague would not reach from the dead, decomposing under the sun in the courtyards of the cloisters, to the living, crouching fearfully in the Prior's Garden—carried there by flies, birds, and lizards? Or, what was worse, by means of the age-old carriers of the plague—rats, which nested in the granaries and larders and in the basements crowded with vats and barrels of wine between the garden and the *Chiostro Piccolo*. The look-out tower, built a hundred years before, after the Certosa's destruction by the pirates, was useless now. The new invader would not approach from the sea, nor was there any way to observe its approach from the interior of the island. It had been within the precincts of the fortress itself for a month.

Only pride, that enemy of humility with which the tunic is sewn, prevented the monks, backed against their own wall of defense, from admitting their error, opening the gates of the Certosa, and crossing with heads bent in repentance the bulwark of corpses that divided them from the flood of tears and suffering that had inundated the island. The monks waited for an excuse. It came in the second half of September. The number of deaths had diminished in the first days of September, and the islanders had taken heart at the sight of two new wayside chapels, which on the advice of the bishop of the island had been built in honor of Saint Roche and Saint Sebastian, patrons of the plague-stricken. But immediately afterward, a terrible thing happened: the only three priests on the island died one after the other in the course of a week. Terror gripped the faithful and froze the blood in their veins.

Was it a sign of Providence warning of new devastations to come? Had they not already paid a high enough price for their sins, that now they could not even hear the church bells, that now they would have to die without the sacraments and reveal without the sacraments this atrocious world to the newborn?

It was then that the bishop of the island wrote a letter to the prior of the Certosa humbly imploring him to let three or four monks come out to take the place of the dead priests. The prior's reply is preserved in the archives. In succinct terms (how insatiable pride is when it has a chance to hide its secret weakness and save itself!) he consented in the name of the brothers entrusted to his care *di ponere la vita per il prossimo nonostante che sia ministerio repugnante alla nostra professione*, to offer their lives for their neighbors even though it be a ministry repugnant to the order.

The morning of September 19, the gates of the Certosa opened. Four monks slowly crossed the threshold. Swaying above their heads on a hastily built wooden litter was the famous *Pietà dell'Isola*, the work of an unknown Sienese master acquired by the monastery in the sixteenth century to commemorate an anniversary of its foundation. In the kinder September sun every color of the worn polychrome acquired its full tone: the golden tresses of the *Mater Dolorosa* shone, and only the long thin body of the Son seemed grayer, as if it had been sprinkled with ashes before coming into the light of day. In the chapel of the Certosa echoed the silvery thin voice of the little bell. The Certosini stopped for a moment and glanced at the malevolent faces of the group of passersby that stopped suddenly. But seeing that it was vain to hope someone would take the sacred weight from their shoulders in sign of reconciliation, the monks moved on toward the main church, often stopping along the way and drying the rivulets of perspiration on their foreheads with the sleeves of their habits. When they reached the end of their Calvary, they celebrated mass and remained among the inhabitants of the island. In October, as the last embers of the plague were extinguished, two of the monks really "offered their lives for their neighbor." But neither then nor later was anything able to erase in the islanders' eyes the ignominy of "the order that had found that ministry repugnant." And more than one brick was added to the wall that was to separate the Certosa from the island for centuries to come by the fact that those whose hearts had trembled in helpless fear in the face of the scourge now found courage enough in those same hearts to reach out their hands when there was an opportunity for material gain: by virtue of the ancient Angevin grant, the Certosa received all the island possessions that had been deprived by the contagion of their legal proprietors and natural heirs.

Thus the Certosa reached the end of its glorious and tempestuous history, the end decreed by Joseph Bonaparte and accepted with relief by the island. All attempts to restore it failed, and the slow decadence that the new epoch prepared for it truly could not have been sadder: first it was turned into a prison, then into an asylum for invalids and cripples, and, finally, in 1860, into a barracks for a discipline company of the army. Where the quiet of prayer and cloistered abundance had once existed for centuries, there now sounded, in succession, the rosaries of convicts, the din of wooden legs tapping and the hissing of imprecations, the metallic clatter of arms and the rustling sound of soldiers' curses. And perhaps those sounds were more pleasing to the God of the plague, the God who sent ill fortune to man constantly to remind his disaccustomed feet of the thorns and sharp stones of our terrestrial wandering, than the click of monastic sandals in the shade of the porticoes of the *Chiostro Grande* and the *Chiostro Piccolo*, the jingle of ducats in the money-bags of the Certosa, and the terrified whispers of whitened lips in the refuge of the *Giardino del Priore*.

But the Certosa was restored—not, to be sure, in its former splendor, but it was restored—on the eve of the First World War. With the consent of the island authorities four monks came from a monastery between Pisa and Lucca. Having become acquainted with the history of the Certosa, they decided of their own free will that every year on September 19, they would humbly bend their shoulders under the sculpture of the *Pietà dell'Isola* and carry it in procession to the church and back again, as if in symbolic atonement for the sin of their predecessors of 1656. There was a tacit understanding that no one except the monks was to touch the handles of the litter on which the Mother of Sorrows held in her arms the inanimate body of the Redeemer. If one of the monks died, another came from the mainland to take his place. The *festa* of September 19 quickly established itself and became an indivisible part of the life of the inhabitants of the island. In the first years, because of the war, perhaps one saw in the sculpture of the Sienese master not only a reminder of the episode that had taken place two and a half centuries before but also the image of a woman lifting from the battlefield the mortal remains of a father, husband, or son. Later the islanders certainly discovered the attraction to tourists of that ceremony, which stamped an exotic seal on the end of the visitors' season in the island. The Second World War probably renewed that eloquence which the *Pietà dell'Isola* had had during the preceding war. But to all these elements must be added the most important one. In the south of Italy, where human solitude before God and Nature, in the presence of the secret of Life and Death, finds its delight in miracles, and in the folk magic of the Lucanian and Calabrian countryside, in the power of the *iettatura*, of the *malocchio*, of the breaking of spells, in the miraculous skulls of the Neapolitan catacombs of Santa Maria della Sanità, in the dramatic processions of the Passion, in the gloomy realism of the instruments of the Passion of Our Lord carried about on Easter eve in Sicily and Sardinia—in this south, a singular coincidence of date must have caught the attention of the island, because every year on September 19 the miracle of San Gennaro takes place in nearby Naples. It is tempting to imagine that above the bay a kind of signal immediately passed between the crowd on the island that followed the procession from the Certosa and the crowd that cheered and applauded the same day in Naples at the news that the coagulated blood of the martyr saint of Pozzuoli had again liquefied.

The Certosa was poor now and had lost all its former wealth. With difficulty its new residents planted a small vineyard in the wild and ruined Prior's Garden. Every day one of the monks took an alms-bag and went begging among the passengers of the boat than ran between the island and Naples, and among the passersby on the streets of Naples as well. The monks did not have even the means to remove the ruins inside the walls of the Certosa. Only the wall itself, cracked and broken in so many places, was more or less restored to its original state in 1933 (seventeen years before the events with which the present narrative will be concerned) by the best *mastro* on the island, Sebastiano. It was Sebastiano's last major work: shortly before completing it the tragedy occurred, and for some time, under the influence of Immacolata, the inhabitants of the island again looked on the Certosa with superstitious rancor.

What else is there to describe? The Certosa, its famous sculpture, and, at the end of this chapter, the island itself seen from on high, from the summit of Monte della Madonna dei Marini.

From a distance the Certosa suggests a gray fortress, heavy and massive, but from nearby, there is little, except its size, that distinguishes it from the architecture of the whole island. All the roofs on the island are vaults that look like wooden shovel faces turned upside-down—a memento of the times when water was provided by the rains and conducted through drains laid out around the vaults of the roofs into receptacles on the ground. Today only a second function is served by the hemispherical vaults of the roofs: the sun's heat is diffused over the largest possible surface. The clock tower, like the other little turrets on the island, is topped by a triangular slanted hood.

The unknown sculptor of the *Pietà dell'Isola* must have carefully studied the sculptures and pictures of his predecessors and contemporaries on the same theme before he applied his chisel to wood. The *Pietà* has no originality. The position of the Mother at once suggests the classicizing Michelangelo of the Basilica of St. Peter, before he created the dramatic forms of the Palestrina *Pietà* and the *Pietà* of the Cathedral of Florence. In the figure of Christ, instead of the tradition of the body bent delicately like a ribbon between the outstretched arms, an older tradition is preserved: the body is rigid and tense in an almost abstract plane. The face of the Madonna framed in golden tresses slipping out from under the black kerchief that falls to her shoulders is sad and yet strangely serene, as in Perugino's San Giusto *Pietà*. Her eyes and mouth seem to unite in a kiss on the lips of the Son, half open in pain and thirst. One would like to believe that the Sienese master had read the *Laudi* of the thirteenth-century Jacopone da Todi, and that while he worked he often repeated to himself these two verses: *una han sepoltura . . . mate e filio affocato* and *de dura morte afferrate . . . mate e filio a un cruciato*: "Mother and Son have the same tomb" and "grasped by one cruel death . . . together in the Crucifixion of pain."

When Padre Rocca, who comes from Mantua, looks out over the island in the last rays of the setting sun from the belvedere near his little church and parish, he always makes the same mental observation (even though he has already spent thirty years on the island): "On the surface it is the typical Mediterranean landscape, just as the Romantic painters and poets of the beginning of the last century saw it and represented it; but if you look for a while at the sweet, ripe shadows of the rocks and trees and houses sprinkled with a gilding of light, and trembling in the brief purple reflection of the sea, you realize that there is something of the classical in it as well."

III

Sebastiano was thirty years old when he was commissioned to repair the wall of the Certosa. He was born on the island, the only son of a fisherman who rowed tourists to the Green Grotto during the season. Both of his parents died when he was young, and Sebastiano inherited his father's boat and two professions. After he finished his military service in Livorno and Florence, he sold the boat and the nets, rented out his parents' house near Monte del Faro, and moved to Naples to learn the mason's craft. He stayed there five years, working first as an assistant mason and later as a young *mastro* on the removal of the baroque adornments of the Flemish-Gothic church of Santa Maria Donnaregina in the old quarter of the city.

Sebastiano returned to the island and soon became famous for his skill in his craft and for his conscientiousness in the execution of his work. Although the building boom on the island (which had lasted throughout the preceding century, when English and German travelers "discovered" the island) had long since entered a phase of gradual decline, Sebastiano never waited long for a job while he passed his time in the house at the foot of the lighthouse or in the bar in the square. The modest local commissions, however, did not much attract him. He had seen the churches of Florence during his military service, and he had worked in Naples, where he would pass his lunch hour in the cool nave of Donnaregina—with his eyes ecstactically fixed on the tomb of Maria of Hungary, the work of the chisel of Tino di Camaino, and on Cavallini's frescoes—or in the Loffredo Chapel, adorned with frescoes by followers of Giotto and Cimabue. Then Sebastiano had dreamed of another kind of work. But there was probably no expecting it on the island, so in his free moments he would sit in the courtyard of his house and carve bas-reliefs from the stone that was so common on the island. For the most part he sculptured fruit-laden *carrettini* with two enormous wheels drawn by oxen, or strange fish shapes and smaller boats, or figures of archers and centaurs like those he had seen many times on the metopes of Thesauros sul Sele and at Paestum, and he would carve scenes of the Passion. The imaginative world of the self-taught sculptor, who barely knew how to read and write, was stretched like a tent on these four pegs: the ancient methods of fruit harvesting still practiced here and there in the Sorrentine peninsula and in the Salernitano, as well as in Sicily and Sardinia; fishing; the Greek representations of war and history; and the pictures that, in Florentine and Neapolitan churches, in the church in the square, and in the little chapel on Monte della Madonna dei Marini, made people kneel and bend their heads to their breasts as the sweet breeze bends the heavy ears of grain in their sheaves. In a certain way that was the instinctive world of imagination of the whole island.

But as soon as Sebastiano returned from Naples and set his string-tied suitcase on his native soil, all his thoughts turned toward the Certosa.

The monks were in no position to consider any kind of restoration; their money barely sufficed to provide for the most urgent daily needs. Sebastiano visited them often. He would silently caress the wounded columns of the *Chiostro Grande*, expertly measure the damage to the walls of the buildings, sit thoughtfully on the little mounds of rubbish swept under the porticoes, and, before leaving, slowly make the circuit of the outer walls. He was loved at the Certosa, perhaps because he was the only person on the island who loved the Certosa.

In the meantime he waited patiently, and again he

became attached to the places of his childhood and youth.

Below his house, which seemed almost to be glued to the declivity of Monte del Faro, there was a little green valley with enough grass to attract the nearby flocks of black goats and sheep. The three shepherd boys slept when it was hot, and when there was a breeze they played *morra*, screeching like hoot owls as they sat under a large nut tree in a hollow of the valley. Above, on the rocky heights that cut off the view of the sea, the stone remains of one of the Roman villas bleached in the sun like the calcified bones of a skeleton. A path leads to the ruins through scattered rye patches dotted with poppies, a path bordered at every step by a living hedgerow of aloe and by dead cactus leaves. Hunters sat motionless in some of the dips of the path with dogs that hunted with their eyes for quail in the vicinity of Monte del Faro; more often the dogs' gaze caught the gulls that skimmed the surface of the water in rapid descent and sometimes rebounded in a single motion above the high line of the shore. The island was beautiful, more beautiful now than when as a boy Sebastiano had known all its secret hiding places. It lulled itself to the sound of the crickets. It lazily followed the strips of shadow across the face of the sundial. At dawn it shone with freshness. In full day it put on a thin veil of heat. In the late afternoon it revealed itself in all the sharpness of its outline as far as distant Naples. At night the island was full of secret rustlings, chattering, loud bursts of laughter, murmurings, and echoes. It breathed continually in a tepid atmosphere of the past: it had preserved the echoes of past epochs in nature and in its ruins. Returning home at night

Sebastiano would pass beside the deep cavern where the moon had once shone on the mysteries of the Romans: the dance of those naked boys and girls whose image was immortalized in the scene of the cavalcade in the bas-relief discovered at Monte della Madonna dei Marini. Hurrying and feeling his way along the path that wound around the back wall of the Certosa, Sebastiano automatically made the sign of the cross at the thought of the bodies of the plague-stricken that had been thrown into the cloister from there.

Then there was Immacolata who lived on the island.

IV

Immacolata was the daughter of the widow of a stone quarrier at Capo Scogliera. Soon after Sebastiano returned from Naples to the island, he went to the quarry near her house to look for building stone. It was then that he saw Immacolata for the first time. She was eighteen.

He paid little attention to the blocks of stone torn out of the walls of the promontory and rolled to the edge of the road, he was so absorbed by the sight of the young woman who led him to her two brothers, who continued the trade of their father. How was it that he had never noticed her before, when she was still a girl or at the funeral of her father, crushed to death by the premature explosion of a dynamite charge at the bottom of the quarry? She was not genuinely beautiful, but there was something elementally physical in her whole being. She moved with the ease and grace of a young animal, as if she were fully aware of arousing desire in men at every agile and slightly somnolent movement of her body. Most of all Sebastiano liked her hair, which glittered like bronze and was so rare on the island, where women vied with each other only in their various shades of raven-black hair.

After that, he went to see Immacolata every Sunday after sunset, and in the summer they would disappear among the ginestra bushes that formed a broad plain sloping up beyond the quarry and grew halfway up Monte del Sole. She knew every stone there, every crevice in the ground, for since the death of her father she had come this way every day to do the cleaning for Padre Rocca. In the hot evenings they would lie in the grass mouth to mouth with their arms around each other; or they would lie on their backs next to each other, their gaze wandering among the stars, hard and glassy over their heads, pale lower in the sky, and glimmering with an uncertain light over the distant glow of Naples. Then they would go to her house for a glass of wine. One morning Sebastiano woke earlier than usual; he got up before dawn, opened the front door, sat down on the stoop, and looked at the last stars, like morning dew on the leaves of trees and flowers. And he regretted that he was not watching them with Immacolata. He talked to her mother, and the wedding was arranged for three years later.

That year, 1933, life seemed to smile on him from two sides at once: in a couple of months, on the holiday of the *Pietà dell'Isola*, he would lead Immacolata to the altar, and in April the monks had finally decided on the restoration of the Certosa, beginning with the walls.

It was an unforgettable moment on the island when Sebastiano nailed up the planks of a movable scaffolding under the wall of the Certosa and dug a pit outside the *Chiostro Grande* to slake lime. A crowd of men dressed in black and women with colored scarves on their heads gathered at a distance, commenting in whispers on the event. Four monks wearing dark brown habits tied with white cords at the waist, with their hoods hanging halfway down their backs, followed all of Sebastiano's movements in silent attention. Step by step the children accompanied little Tonino, whom Sebastiano had long since taken as his helper from the poorest village at the port. So many years had passed since the duel between the Certosa and the island, yet the restoration of that wall made a greater and somehow more real impression on the islanders than had the return of the monks before the First World War. The new inhabitants of the Certosa secretly nurtured the hope that the trowel of the best *mastro* on the island would also heal, in addition to the breaches and cracks in the wall, the still-open wound of the past; and this is surely why the Certosa, although it had always been proud of its gray-green color, like the patina of the rocks along the shore, chose to see the restored walls painted the calcium white of all the houses and fences on the island. For almost three centuries the generations of inhabitants of the island had been unwilling to abandon to the winds of forgetfulness the last crumbs of mistrust that local history had passed down from father to son and son to grandson to their hands, outstretched over the abyss of time.

Sebastiano stood alone on his scaffolding, out of reach of these waves of ancient wrath and equally ancient prayers for pardon that turned and rebounded from each other. At last he could look as much as he liked at the rays of sunlight playing in and out of the colonnades. And somewhere above him he heard music such as no human ears had ever heard. He gazed at the panes in the windows of the chapel, and he saw pictures that human eyes had never seen; at the palms in the Prior's Garden, which beat the sky with their green fronds, and he remembered the *Chiostro del Paradiso* from his two-day pilgrimage to Amalfi; and at the cracks in the half-closed little windows of four cells of the cloister building, through which only God could catch and gather up to Himself the slender thread of a prayer. Sebastiano often turned back in memory to the years he had spent at Donnaregina. Again he felt like a mason in the service of centuries that he could never understand and before which his spirit trembled. Had it not been for centuries the destiny and glory of man to leave behind him as enduring as possible a sign of his hand? And although it would not have been difficult for Sebastiano to finish the wall of the Certosa in three months' time, he had already conceived the idea of prolonging the work at least till the middle of September.

Similarities of human destinies are deceptive. Yet it is impossible to resist the impression that Sebastiano, driven by an unknown force, had entered on a trail carved out several hundred years before by the history of the unfortunate founder of the Certosa and buried all these centuries in the sand of a world that rolls ever onward. For both of them, though for different reasons and in different circumstances, the Certosa was to have been a crown of triumph. And for both of them, still in different circumstances, it became a crown of thorns. Since time immemorial philosophers have debated whether life repeats itself, like an unimaginative needleworker embroidering the same patterns over and over again, and the issue is still unresolved. Whether the inscrutable sentences of God are written in thousands of copies and modified only in the smallest details, or whether, in the opposite view, each of us is reflected in the immense eye of Providence and receives from the infallible hand of the Judge a different fate tailored exclusively to his measure is a question that troubles believers and theologians. But even though Immacolata burdened the Certosa with too much responsibility for the misfortune that befell her and Sebastiano, the poor mason of Monte del Faro seems at a certain point to have entered a path covered over for ages and to have stumbled on the petrified bones of the prince-secretary of Joan of Anjou hidden in the sand.

That moment came in July, the twenty-fifth to be exact. The wall was just about finished, and Sebastiano was working unhurriedly on the last section. Built behind the Prior's Garden right over the declivity of the plateau on the sea side, it was the most difficult section. The sun blazed mercilessly, its heat unrelieved by even a breath of wind, and permitted the trees to throw no more leaf shadow on the scorched ground than there are dots stamped on summer percales. From afar the shore rocks looked as dry as pumice. The sky was undone by the heat, like tissue paper stuck to a heated pot. There was nothing extraordinary in the fact that Sebastiano set about slaking fresh lime during his lunch break. The dust and white smoke over the pit blended with the milky-white atmosphere that enveloped the island. There was no one around; Tonino had taken the funicular down to the port. From time to time the wooden click of sandals on the stone walks of the nearby cloister could be heard.

In that solitude and quiet, broken only by the hissing of the lime, Sebastiano suddenly looked up and saw Immacolata at a bend in the road above, coming toward him from town.

A half-hour later the clock in the square struck

one. The lonely sound floated over the island, describing ever larger and more muffled circles; Tonino hurried off from the funicular station toward the Certosa. The last vibration of the clock's echo had barely died out when the air, motionless again, resounded to a man's heart-rending scream, which gave way at once to a howl or a whine, not exactly like a wild beast's but not human either, a long, drawn-out and painful wail. Then a weakening pause and the wail, quieter now, was overpowered by another sound, as if suddenly torn from all the cords—the piercing scream of a woman. When Tonino finally emerged from the path in front of the Certosa, he saw Immacolata staggering toward him. She had buried her hands in her magnificent bronze hair and was pressing them to her temples. When she saw Tonino she screamed twice, *Aiuto, aiuto*! She stopped suddenly, clutched her stomach, and sank to a sitting position on the ground. Tonino stopped by her only a fraction of a second and then ran on. By the lime pit two monks were kneeling over a figure twisted in convulsions, a human tatter soaked with white powder and lying face down on the ground frantically jabbing his hands into his eyes. The three of them finally managed to turn him over on his back: small cracked flecks of lime still stuck to his hands, his cheeks, and his forehead. Sebastiano's face was swollen and red; locked like claws his fingers continually tried to cover his eyes; he pressed them with a panting groan down into the orbits. Finally the monks and Tonino managed (Sebastiano did not offer much resistance) to carry him to the cloister *ambulatorio* in the *Chiostro Piccolo*. Running to town for the doctor, Tonino passed Immacolata still sitting on the ground, rhythmically swaying back and forth and softly repeating: *aiuto, aiuto*! But it was not clear whether she was repeating that cry for help to herself or to the little crowd of people around her that her shout had brought from their houses in the most violent heat of the afternoon.

Slowly Immacolata calmed herself enough to utter something more than her monotonous call for help. She told the *carabinieri* sergeant that Sebastiano had tripped and struck his knee on the long handle of the shovel he used to slake the lime: the curved shovel, shallowly immersed in the pit, had snapped back like a bolt of lightning and splashed its entire contents in his face. The two monks listened to this account with lowered eyelids—eyelids under which obstinately persisted the sight of the wooden handle not leaning on the side of the square pit where Sebastiano had writhed in pain. But could one be sure that the shovel, forcefully struck by his knee, had not bounced to the opposite side of the pit? Then the rotation of the shovel face in the direction of Sebastiano's head would have been even more comprehensible. For the moment the matter would have to stand there, until Sebastiano could speak. But days and weeks passed, and Sebastiano lay motionless in the penumbra of what had once been a monk's cell with the upper part of his head bandaged and a bandage over his eyes and mouth, as if gagged.

The procession of the *Pietà dell'Isola* was sad that year. Fewer fireworks were set off, and those grudgingly. The crowd of people on the road from the Certosa to the church watched with embarrassment the little group bearing the statue; the children tossed flowers and streamers less abundantly than usual, and then hid behind the row of adults. The procession itself tried to move along as fast as it could. At sunset only the façade of the church in the square was illu-

minated. Had the old shadow come back to life? Did
people believe the accusations made by Immacolata,
who ever since the accident had cursed the Certosa
from afar? Did they think of the gray patch in the
white-plastered wall of the Certosa that was visible
from the sea behind the Prior's Garden? Did they look
at the Madonna, with her glance suspended over the
lips of the tortured Son, and remember that only a
week before Immacolata had given birth to a dead
child, which Padre Rocca (although she belonged to
a different parish) baptized, christened Giovanni, and
buried in the cemetery at the foot of Monte della
Madonna dei Marini?

On the way back the procession broke up before
reaching the gate of the Certosa. Beyond the gate,
in the courtyard of the *Chiostro Grande*, the four
monks stopped dumbfounded and set down their load
at what they saw. Between the columns of the portico,
barefoot and wearing only trousers and a shirt and
with his head bandaged, walked Sebastiano. He did
not answer when called, nor did he make even the
slightest movement of his head. As he walked he
touched the columns with outstretched hands, as if he
were groping. The monks were sure he was deaf. Perhaps he was mute. And he was probably blind.

V

The four monks were mistaken. When Sebastiano
emerged from the cell on September 19, 1933, after
eight weeks of mortal torpor, he was not altogether
deaf, nor altogether mute, nor altogether blind. The
shock of the accident by the Certosa wall had only
robbed him of hearing and speech to such a degree
that the words imprisoned in his throat were too

weak to break out and preferred to silence their timidly beating little hearts rather than to break into flight with the despairing hum of broken wings. And the sounds of the world around him were not altogether dead and incomprehensible, but reduced to the buzz of a seashell held up to the ear; they seemed to reach him as if through a thick pane of glass. His left eye was forever covered by an immovable membrane, but there remained a little crack in the corner of his right eye. If he lifted his head at an angle he saw persons and objects in an incessant vibration, as they are when you turn from an afternoon nap and look at the sun from under blinking eyelashes: even the fluctuating shadows are split into an infinite number of smaller shadows, leading one's shattered attention even farther from its real source.

One may wonder whether these three faculties of human existence, of which Sebastiano had been in large measure deprived, were of any use to him at all. For Sebastiano had lost something else more important then hearing, speech, or sight: his memory. The last and only sensation that he salvaged from the world was pain. Pain so horrible that the mere recollection of it raised the empty lump of a moan in his throat and shook him for a long time, as if he were hiccuping. He was frightened by everything; the mere touch of a tree, a house, or a passerby drove him to panic. Somewhere deep inside him, under the lowest stratum of this pain, there crawled a grim suffering without a face, without a name, and without associations. There were moments when he was oppressed, rather than by the suffering itself, by its insinuation, never identified and in its dark formlessness constantly eluding his outstretched arms. How much more painful was the blindness of his memory than the blindness of his eyes! And how much more tormenting was the shadow of a shadow of his memory fleeing farther and farther from its source than the half-mute apparitions, the tattered fragments and fleeting forms that sparkled and whirled in an eternal dance before his half-closed eyelid!

For the first two or three days a curious group, mostly children, kept him company in his wanderings far and wide over the island. They quickly realized that every effort to bring him back to the past was useless, but they feared that on the treacherous narrow paths along the edge of the precipice he might step into that future from which there is no return. He always walked barefoot ahead of them, and sometimes he broke into a short dash as if he sensed that he were being followed. Then he would stop, listen intently, and, unable to distinguish the human voices from the murmur of the sea, sit down peacefully. Then his escort too would stop behind him; they discussed whether they should leave him to his fate; they wondered (although the September sun was milder) whether they should put a fisherman's straw hat on his head.

Although Sebastiano had no determined goal, he rarely rested, constantly driven on by an obtuse perseverance that was an end in itself. But the island had no straight roads: they all ran around it or crossed it, returning like rope knots to where they had begun. So he appeared several times a day in the same places, everywhere received by the silent gaze of the men and the tearful compassion of the women. The first day toward evening he fell exhausted on a bench in the village at the foot of Monte della Madonna dei Marini and began moving his lips voicelessly like a fish thrown up on the sand. A kettle of milk was brought to him, a plate of soup, and a half loaf of bread. From then on, whenever he stopped at that hour near human habitation, he did not lack for food.

The bird of misfortune that soars over the immense world had singled out a victim on the island; and the island, as accustomed to misfortune as it was to the algae that settle on the seashore after low tide and dry in the sun until they decay, bent in silent resignation over the victim abandoned half-alive by his celestial assailant.

The curious abandoned the wanderer when the sun set behind a nearby island and the fan of night, still slightly reddened along the broad shore, rose from the sea. Sebastiano slept in the open air, and even the darkness, suddenly whisking away the tremor of light and shadow before his half-open lid, startled him. He bedded himself as he could: on the hard, naked earth under a hanging rock, in the cool caverns, in the grass between the roots of trees, in the hard stubble of the ginestra, or, more happily than elsewhere, on the fine, warm sand of the beaches, but never within the orbit of human habitation. At dawn he took to the beaten paths and looked for the nearest spring.

He never avoided the Certosa in his wanderings, and when he went around it and seemed to touch the wall with aversion, it was at first taken as a sign that innumerable fragments of memory rattled around inside him. To all appearances, however, he did not recognize his own house by Monte del Faro, and the first time he passed through the village of the stone-cutters and Immacolata ran out into the road and fell down with loud sobs at his knees, vainly calling him by name, he was so frightened that he fled and ran off with long leaps in the direction of Capo Scogliera.

Only at the entrance to the stone quarry did he recover from his fright, and walking more slowly then, he turned into a path leading to the ruins of the Roman villa. That day Immacolata joined his sad retinue. She returned home that evening overcome by what she had seen. From then on, every time she noticed him from a distance, a rapid sign of the cross that ended with her thumb timidly held to her lips was the only acknowledgment she made of their former engagement.

It could be said that Sebastiano had retained more memory of all the roads and paths on the island in his naked feet than in that relic of sight which fate had spared him. He remembered every irregularity, every smooth and even stretch of stone paving, every rock, every tree stump and every grassy zone in the valleys, every rise and every hollow in the mule paths that traversed the slopes of the uplands. In the chaos of his mind and heart only one sensation—feeling again and so well recognizing the earth under his feet— sometimes touched his mouth with a cheerful smile. Then he would walk straight ahead without fatigue, and he seemed to hear through the humming in his ears a pure and reassuring note from somewhere below. Perhaps in some mysterious way the blood in his veins picked up the rhythm of the secret pulsation of the island on which he had been born and which he had once loved with a conscious love.

After those first few days the group that accompanied him slowly began to disperse, until they altogether deserted him. Assured that he had at least retained the sensitivity of his feet after the accident and that life was dearer to him than death, the inhabitants of the island entrusted him to the protection of God and Providence. He remained alone then with his nameless suffering and his blinded memory, which only once roused him with a sudden expressiveness like the lightning puncture of a needle: the first night, from his lair at the foot of Monte della Madonna dei Marini, he saw a luminous spot vibrating in the distance.

It was the façade of the church in the square, illuminated in honor of the feast of the *Pietà dell'Isola.*

VI

Months passed, and then years, and the island became accustomed to its solitary wanderer. With the passing of time Sebastiano was seen even more rarely. Often he disappeared and several days would pass before he unexpectedly re-emerged as if from underground, now here, now there, with his little sack of belongings, sewn from old sailcloth. Autumn and winter, always barefoot, he paid no attention to the cold or to the rain as he waited patiently on the edge of some inhabited zone until someone finally noticed him from the window. But in bad weather he sought a different refuge for the night: under a surviving piece of roof in the Roman ruins, under the covered verandas of villas empty after the season, in the entrance hall of a square dwelling by the lighthouse. The *carabinieri*'s attempt to put him in the little hospice on the island ended unsuccessfully; that was the only time that anyone had seen him angry, and fragments of a strange stutter came from his mouth. Since he was not a threat to public order, the next day the door to that sad liberty of wandering was again opened for him. The first winter the question of his memory was again briefly raised (in a negative manner this time), for even the cold was unable to drive him at night either behind the walls of the Certosa or to his own little house, which the authorities finally turned over indefinitely to a school of ornamental crafts. Slowly, no one knew how or when, the moment arrived when it seemed that the former Sebastiano had never existed—only, from time immemorial, that miserable creature into whose hands tourists, newly arrived and still unfamiliar with the life of the island, slid an offering that he immediately rejected. *Er ist verrückt,* the Germans said in horror. "He doesn't seem to be in need," said the English, shrugging their shoulders. Slowly, too, the feast that ended the season regained its former splendor.

It is time to describe Sebastiano's appearance. Before the accident he was of average height. He had broad shoulders and a square angular head that might have been carved from some hard wood. Like a visor his low forehead covered large greenish eyes in which calm and vigor were mixed with a childlike ingenuousness. Eight weeks in bed at the Certosa aged him ten years. He came out thin and flabby, as if the bones were trying to break through the envelope of skin. That abrupt advance in age had changed him in two ways: Sebastiano seemed taller than before, but at the same time strangely bent forward because of the vulture-like curve of his back and neck. The features of his face were drawn and pulled from the burn, especially on the right side. His eyes, one sealed and the other underscored by an oblique crack, gave him an expression of feigned or impotent ferocity. He had become partially bald in those two months. His sparse hair seemed longer and wilder and had to be confined in a round knot at the back of his neck. In compensation he had a thick curly beard like the ancient busts of Greek sages or the Apostles in Byzantine frescoes. Now and then the shepherds cut Sebastiano's hair while he slept, when he came to the little green valley where the sheep and goats fattened. He liked to sleep to the barely perceptible sound of the little Abruzzi hornpipe that the shepherds sometimes carried with them. Other than the secret voice of the earth beneath the soles of his feet, this was the only clear, distinct, and pain-relieving note that penetrated his consciousness.

Among the places he particularly favored during his roaming about the island were these: the rarely frequented slopes of Monte della Madonna dei Marini, to the east; Capo Scogliera, on the sea side; and a shallow pool between the twin-peaked rock rising from the bottom of the sea just offshore and the western slope of Monte del Faro. On the wild slope of the mountain, the holly growing in thin layers of soil on the rocks, the high-stemmed flowers, and the soft networks of bindweed formed a spot in which a seated man was completely covered. There the sunrise struck the island with its first rays and powdered the air with a dew of light. The breath coursed through the body like a fresh stream, and it was like pressing lips to a cool spring before turning again to the dry burst of solar heat. On a mound of sand by the sea at Capo Scogliera, covered halfway up by stones, a black cross commemorated the death of nine fishermen in a storm at the beginning of the century. Few people reached here from the mainland, for the only access meant frequent sliding over the rocks, while the black monument of the catastrophe held boats at bay. Like Sebastiano, the seagulls that roosted on the arms of the cross, indifferent to the explosions from the stone quarries, preferred this secluded spot to all others. In the summer Sebastiano bathed in the pool between the two-peaked rock and Monte del Faro. Without undressing he entered the water above his waist and immersed his head. The emerald-green spots of stones, the dark-red marine musk, the roses and blues of algae branches, laces to which little shells were glued, the silver flashes of tiny sardines—he saw everything through the crack in his eye with such clarity, as if only the underwater kingdom were unveiled to him. Perhaps it was for this that he preferred that pool above all else. He would dry himself on the flat protuberance of the rock wall, and sometimes he would still be lying there long after sunset, when the revolving fire began its nightly rotation in the glass tower of the lighthouse. Sebastiano's world, the island he traversed unceasingly, was like a clock the two hands of which advanced together around the quadrant and innumerable times crossed the same segments of division, subject only to the rhythms of the toothed cogs in the covered mechanism. A clock does not ask if it is night or day, spring or autumn. Its time is dead, the skeleton of time. Unless it is filled like modeled clay with living hours, months, and years, it remains immobile despite all appearance of motion. It is like a river dried up by drought: it winds along the ribbon of its desiccated bed, it keeps its former shape and direction, it still courses around the sharp turns and sweet meanderings, but it has already forgotten what water is—talking with tens of voices, changing into tens of colors, reflecting the sky in its passage, and reflecting the trees and clouds.

If Sebastiano had been able to consider his own life, he would have discovered that he really never knew when he awoke from sleep: at dawn, when the luminous ray before his right eye lifted his body from his mat; or past the threshold of night, when darkness and fatigue laid him on the ground and made him impotent with their weight. During the day he wandered about the island as if asleep. And he sank into the expanses of nocturnal dreams as if in waking. Under the wings of night and sleep, his blind eyes opened and found in the desert of memory a few oases in the hardened lava crust: Maria of Hungary, lying carved in stone on her tomb in the Church of Donnaregina, leaned on one elbow and drew her face toward his; Cavallini's Madonna, wearing the medallion of the Infant on her breast and to her right the angel that defends her from the assault of the dragon; golden-haired cherubim that fly down from the walls and circle so closely that they fill him with terror as well as excitement; fruit-laden carts pulled by oxen with human heads; a black cross torn from a mound of earth and carried by someone up a mountain. A casual witness leaning over the sleeping man would also have heard sounds that resembled words and short sobs or sighs. At daybreak everything disappeared without the slightest trace, like the flame on the altar when it is extinguished by the tin cone of the snuffer.

One day at the beginning of summer 1939, he woke up at dawn on the slope of Monte della Madonna dei Marini and, instead of going as usual to the well by the gate of the little cemetery where Padre Rocca had buried Immacolata's son, he began to climb up toward the top. The holly branches hurt him as he went. The hard thistle stalks and the bending flower stems struck him like whips, but he did not stop. Gripping the protruding ridges of the slope, he climbed upward, driven on by a strange sense of exaltation and urgency. Until then he had always instinctively gone around the place where the Madonna of Seafarers watched, although on rainy nights he might venture as far as the lower floors of Roman villas. That day, however, instinct guided his steps another way. The sun had already emerged from its marine covering when he appeared from behind the last projection perpendicular to the wall and stood up on the flat level of the peak. The animated statue with arms bent at the elbow and lifted toward the sky, like a two-armed candlestick, seemed to long for the brightness of dawn. The regular path on the plateau was sufficiently wide and safe that the islanders and the tourists often followed it to the little church or to the ancient ruins. The door of the chapel was half open; the dark crack quivered with a luminous reflection from inside. The coarse cloth curtain hanging in the doorway swelled with a breath of wind.

Sebastiano approached the entrance cautiously and pushed the door open. At first the darkness enveloped him. Then, tilting his head up at an angle, he perceived through a fog two little flaming tongues that quivered against a background of dark, narrow windows. Farther down, to one side, was the small figure of a kneeling boy. At that moment the priest turned from the altar toward the empty nave and lifted his arms. The movement was instantaneous. It should have been only part of a rapid, complete circle, but noticing the new arrival, Padre Rocca turned pale and froze. In that position he resembled the Madonna dei Marini, with his arms still stretched above the bright forms of the candles in the corners. It lasted so long that the boy stepped up to the altar with a questioning gesture. Sebastiano let his head fall on his chest and sank again into darkness. It was a pure black this time, as if the limpid water of the pool under Monte del Faro where he bathed had come up from the darkness to refresh him. Suddenly something came free in him; it seemed as if something had loosened the knot in his throat. A kind of short and fugitive gleam, far away and without reflection, acute and altogether unnerving, penetrated him like a ray of hot and invisible light. Tears slowly fell from his right eye, and he felt their burning rivulet on his cheek until they rolled from his skin into his beard. Suddenly the inseparable companion of his existence disappeared: the memory of pain and beneath it that suffering without a name and without a face. No, he had not returned to the past; the past had been torn from him without a trace. When Padre Rocca approached him after the mass and said, "Welcome to the house of God! Don't you recognize me? I'm the parish priest of the Madonna dei Marini," Sebastiano only heard the usual hum and did not even nod his head. He finally rose from his knees and without noticing the figure standing before him he left the church, again pushing the door open cautiously.

But a certain change had taken place in him: he saw better. Going down the path to the island, he stopped on two different occasions, each time drawn by a patch of landscape. For a long time he gazed at the yellow, sun-scorched hill as if he had never seen it before, with the thin, contorted trunks and dust-faded leaves of its dwarf olives. And later he noticed a little pine forest, where occasional rays of sunlight fell between the thin, light columns of the trees. The second scene suddenly reawakened in him an inexplicable emotion, and he selected the pine forest as his resting place for the night.

From then on Sebastiano was a regular morning visitor (and in the summer the only visitor other than the boy who served at the mass) at the church on Monte della Madonna dei Marini.

VII

The Second World War barely touched the island. But in the first years its existence might have been guessed from the nature of the new arrivals: the French and English tourists stopped coming; among the Italians from the mainland men in uniform predominated; and there were Germans. Italian Jews with sufficient funds, apprehension, and the gift of foresight settled in some of the more deserted parts of the island to wait out the storm in that relatively out-of-the-way place. One of these, Dr. Filippo Sacerdote of Mantua, discovered his old friend and countryman in Padre Rocca and went to live with him in the parish house, spending his time looking after the health of the village at the foot of the mountain. People talked very little and then in whispers of these unusual newcomers, as if they already knew that the Jews' fate would depend on silence.

Thus, the sea again became a protective shield, as it had been almost three centuries before. This time it endured to the end—even when the bombs fell on Naples and, as in the year of the plague, black columns of smoke, trimmed at the bottom by a scissor-edge of fire, rose in the calm Neapolitan sky; when the moon and stars disappeared at night in the scarlet and black sky; the island remained untouched by the fire of destruction. When the war ended in the south of Italy, the funicular began to carry up from the port— instead of Italians and Germans—American, English, French, and Polish officers. And the Jewish fugitives returned to the mainland. When Vesuvius suddenly awakened in April 1944 after a long sleep, the rain of ash was greeted as a sign of expiation; and the last glow of fire over the crater, like a nocturnal brother of the rainbow, was taken as a sign of the reconciliation of heaven and earth. The only mark that the war left behind on the island appeared in the square some time later: a marble slab in honor of the inhabitants of the island who had fallen in the First World War was enriched by a dozen new names. Immacolata's two brothers headed the funeral list, both cited as *caduto per la Patria in Africa*, and their dates were given.

During these four years, when the world was covered with blood and tears and encompassed by fire and suffering, life on the island followed its usual course. Sebastiano still walked the paths barefoot, turned his head up at an angle toward the sun when he stopped to rest, passed the now more numerous groups of passersby, and by his mere presence seemed to prove that nothing had changed there, and that nothing would change as long as the empty blue space cut off on all sides the disturbing human spectacle. Sebastiano's heart was full of a sweet calm since the morning visits to the little church on Monte della Madonna dei Marini had come to be a clear reference point in his wanderings. Since his accident Immacolata had aged prematurely and become ugly (as only southern women can grow old and turn ugly while still young). She had gone to work again when her brothers were called into service, and now worked in back of the bar in the square. The Certosini looked in vain for a chance to erase the shame of their seventeenth-century predecessors in this new, bellicose intervention of God. Nothing happened that could confer more than a symbolic value on the statue the monks carried out of the Certosa every September 19. Nevertheless they could not but notice with a sense of satisfaction that, just as during the First World War, the danger in the air evoked a flicker of frightened and prayerful invocation in the eyes of the crowd when the *Pietà dell'Isola* passed above their heads.

Only to the life of Padre Rocca had the war brought a great change. When Dr. Sacerdote knocked on the door of the parish house in 1942, for a moment the priest did not believe his eyes. His whole youth, everything that over the years had fallen day after day to the bottom of the deep well of memory, returned to him like a long-held breath. "Is it you, Filippo? Is it you?" he stammered, and touched the shoulders and face of his guest with trembling hands. At the end he broke into a weak and moaning sob like the crying of a baby. Leaning his forehead on the doctor's breast, first hugging him close, then pushing him away, he finally abandoned himself, with no more resistance or fear, to images that sprang up from a dark abyss. Their native Mantua with the oblong opening of the square in front of the Palazzo Ducale and the loggias facing it, the maze of streets downtown and the school in the Corso Giulio Romano, the flat lakes like spring floods, the orphan home near the Gonzaga Palazzo del Tè, and Mantegna's greyhounds—Mantua lighted up and slowly went dark before his eyes in the intoxicating perfume of spring, in the weak glimmer of the street-lamps under the dark, high cupola of the night, in the gray-green icy light of Lombard mornings. Padre Rocca had never gone back; shortly after he was ordained, he was sent to the island. That was in 1920. Besides nostalgia and the feeling that he was an outsider, it was the solitude that caused him the most suffering in the eagle's roost of the Roman emperors, where along with the silent Madonna he looked at the sea and the island immersed in the solar heat. Although he was not yet old, nor was it time for him to think of death, he repeated often and willingly a phrase of La Rochefoucauld that he had read somewhere: *Le soleil ni la mort ne se peuvent regarder fixement.* And yet for years and years he had stared at the one and the other and never saw another living soul except the boy who brought provisions up to him and served at the morning mass and Immacolata, who came in the afternoon. Only on Sunday was the church filled with the faithful. Sometimes tourists came up toward sunset to visit the ruins, and Padre Rocca would accompany them just to exchange a couple of words. After the season the inhabitants of the island sometimes came up to take a look at the Madonna of Seafarers. An ailment that made his legs swollen and heavy like barrels kept him from ever going farther than the village at the foot of the mountain when the last sacrament or a funeral required his presence. "Solitude," he murmured, "what an awful thing it is, Filippo. God gives grace, but not company." And suddenly Padre Rocca realized two things: that the Italian word itself, *sole*, the sun, is a part of "solitude"; and, as he rested his head on the breast of a man of another faith, that he had blasphemed.

Dr. Sacerdote was moved too and, taller than his friend, he put his arms around the priest's neck. Persecuted rather by fear of humiliation and insult than by a real and immediate menace to life and liberty, Dr. Sacerdote had found not only an evidently safe haven but the most important thing of all, esteem and friendship. He was an old bachelor and had left no one other than some distant relatives behind in Mantua.

The two men lived together in the parish house. They rarely saw each other during the day, but in the evening they would walk among the ruins, silently admire the panorama from the belvedere, or chat far into the night in the little room that served as a library, where the guest slept. Gradually the doctor got into the habit of sitting in the last row at morning mass; Sebastiano often knelt not far from him. Like the two candles burning on the altar, like the outstretched arms of the gentle Madonna, they both looked down the little nave and found a solace for their wandering feet.

In the deepest recess of his heart, while in shame imploring God's pardon, Padre Rocca prayed that the war would last as long as possible.

VIII

One day in June 1944, Padre Rocca woke as usual before dawn, but instead of getting up at the first sign of consciousness, as was his habit, he fell at once into a half sleep. Under the thin, cracked skin of consciousness he could feel the enormous weight of his body, which sank no further into sleep, however, for it seemed to be bound and held to the surface as if by a dense growth of algae.

The white light of day poured through the window curtain like milk into a glass bowl. The priest made desperate efforts to free himself from the bonds of sleep, but the more he struggled with that unknown force that had immobilized him in the moment of waking, the weaker and more resigned he felt. His perspiration-soaked shirt stuck to his skin and suffocated him; it seemed to crush his chest with an unbearable weight. As he struggled, half-awake, impotent, and breathing heavily, terror gripped him. It was an indefinable terror, not at all specific but sufficiently menacing and deep to wring from his throat a scream that sounded like a deep breath. He had one desperate wish, to open his eyes. At last he succeeded, and the first thing he saw under his opened lids was the little black crucifix on the sunlit wall. He felt even greater terror. He suddenly lost even that minimal sense of time and place which he had found when he broke through the surface of reality. The cross seemed a spider on the wall. He could not distinguish the end of life from the unfathomable depths of death. Free of the mesh that had bound him so tightly, he lost his breath, and with a terror beyond the limits of an agony that allowed neither time nor place for a scream, he began to sink, floating in the last gleams of consciousness like a body carried by underwater currents in no particular direction.

Half an hour later Dr. Sacerdote was beside him. "He must rest," he said to the boy who served the mass, who had come to get him. The boy helped him give the priest an injection. "He'll have to spend a week in bed." "He could have had a long life," the doctor said to himself, "if it hadn't been for this solitude. It's destroying him bit by bit like a cancer."

Dr. Sacerdote pushed the curtain aside and looked out the window. Sebastiano was sitting on the church steps as if waiting for something. Finally he got up, turned his head around, and went off in the direction of the path along which he had climbed at dawn.

The doctor pulled the chair up to the sick man's bed and looked around the room with interest. Beside the wardrobe of lightly polished wood, the kneeling-bench that looked like a child's school desk, and a white iron washbowl with a pitcher under the basin, there was no furniture. An oil lamp was suspended by little chains from the lower frame of a large picture of the Nativity hanging above the bed. There was a small crucifix on the opposite wall. And on the side walls there were two faded little postcards, pinned at the four corners, with brick-colored withered leaves stuffed under their worn edges. One was a scene of Mantua at night, and the other was a cheap reproduction of the *Pietà dell'Isola*.

The weather was sultry, but with no sign of rain. It was one of those mornings on the island that are clear but somehow leaden at the same time, when you can sit for a long time without moving, and for lack of anything better you turn back to your own neglected and incoherent thoughts, which have been obscured as if by low-floating clouds that darken the landscape and only rarely allow you a glimpse of some hitherto unnoticed or unobserved detail.

Dr. Sacerdote suddenly recalled a scene he had witnessed several months earlier. He had given it slight importance at the time, but just as in a narrow space between wandering clouds you notice with so much more distinctness a patch of the landscape barely glanced at before because the rest of the view is so obscured by dark gray veiling, so the doctor saw the scene again with unusual clarity.

It was almost dark as he returned from delivering a baby in the village. A fine drizzle fell, and the drops were scattered in the air like the little jets of the rotating water taps that irrigated the island's vineyards during the drought. Every few minutes he had to clean his glasses, fogged by the dew of the humid spray. It was a winter day, sad and mournful. Just in front of him he saw a stretch of path and, farther up, the woolly tatters in which the mountain—with the Ro-

man ruins, the church, and the watchful Madonna—
wrapped itself when the bitter cold came. At a distance
the sea murmured in a hushed voice. As the doctor
left the village with its yellow window panes glowing
and dripping, a bent shadow wrapped in rags passed
him going in the opposite direction. The doctor recognized his companion of the morning masses. *Buona
sera*, he shouted. He knew it was useless to expect a
reply. He only shouted to drive away the wintry atmosphere, but the silence in which his words were
drowned seemed gloomy and numbing and failed to
quicken his lonely steps.

Before reaching the crossroad from which the
proper pathway up the mountain turned off, the little
road ran alongside the cemetery. It was girdled by a
low, thick wall, white like all the enclosed places on
the island, and looked something like a bastion or a
dam. Walking with his eyes fixed straight ahead, he
often had the feeling, particularly at dusk, that the
crosses on the tombstones were a row of silent figures
standing on tiptoe to watch passersby. But there had
never been anything in that little cemetery to cause a
shiver. All country cemeteries are like that: when
people pass by, they make the sign of the cross with the
natural familiarity of a greeting made to the living
and a thought consecrated to the dead.

The doctor reached the end of the wall and was
about to turn off to the left when a rustle of foliage
too distinct in the silence to be merely a breath of
wind attracted his attention. He stopped and glanced
toward the cemetery. Some time passed before he
succeeded in distinguishing through his cleaned glasses
the figure of his friend in the dark gloom. Padre Rocca
stood over a small tomb overgrown with grass and
marked by a small cross. With one hand, probably

because of his failing legs, he held onto a young tree and shook it back and forth. He held his other hand closed in a fist on his breast, as if he were holding the edges of his unbuttoned coat. For an instant it seemed to the doctor that the tree was shaking the man who leaned against it, and the rustle of the dead leaves was in fact a human sob. Dr. Sacerdote remembered that a visit to the parish cemetery was, in a certain sense, a part of the daily occupations of his friend, and although it seemed a strange hour and unsuitable weather for such a visit, he passed on without making his presence known.

But halfway up, perhaps held back by some obscure fear, he decided to wait. He stopped under a protruding ledge and sat on a bench that had been set in the shade for tourists; he tried to overcome the cold that penetrated him, pulling his hands inside his sleeves. He had to wait a long time for his friend. The two men covered the remaining piece of road together, both reluctant to talk. Several times the breathless priest had to lean for support on the companion who held his arm, and at one point the doctor dragged him along as if he were bearing a wounded man from a battlefield. For the first time then, the enemy that had been furtively insinuating itself into the heart of the priest of the Madonna dei Marini revealed itself openly.

Now the face of the sick man turned a waxen color. Padre Rocca's breath was almost imperceptible; now and then a weak bubble of air formed in front of his gums like the small bubbles that rise from time to time from the bottom of a pond. Sleep again drove him to the limit of consciousness.

The doctor bathed his face, leaden with heat, in the basin, but no sooner had he dried himself and sat down again in the chair than he felt the beating in his temples increase, and again he surrendered to his slow meditations.

What attracted the doctor's attention most of all, as he remembered that scene several months later, was the shadow that passed him near the entrance to the cemetery. Only God, and perhaps no one else, could ever understand why. Looking back he realized that all the time the two men were climbing up the mountain he had been oppressed by the idea that Sebastiano was following them. Where could he have got that idea? He knew almost nothing about that poor wretch. From the beginning he had taken a professional interest in the case, but the unbalanced cripple would not let him come near. Later the doctor became accustomed to Sebastiano's frequent presence at morning mass. The priest spoke of him with reluctance. Once or twice he had muttered, "What does he always come here for?" The doctor had replied jokingly that Sebastiano was simply trying to preserve the honor of the temple that everyone else had forgotten. But the doctor had another, more serious theory on the subject: he believed that the mason saw the two lighted candles on the altar in the darkness of the little church better than he saw anything else, and so he was involuntarily drawn there.

Why then had the doctor imagined that the shadow was following them, unless it was that Padre Rocca had seemed to be fleeing from something and had run ahead without stopping to the very limit of his forces. *Andiamo Filippo, andiamo . . .*

The doctor opened his lids a crack and suddenly had a strange illusion (one of those strange associations of thought that one should never try to explain by the casual affinity of related elements): the pale torso of a naked man pierced by arrows, beads of coagulated blood dripping from their points, the head bent under long hair that fell to the shoulders, and an expression of pain and, at the same time, of celestial rapture in clear upturned eyes. The vision so startled him that he shook himself as if he were waking from a dream.

Some time passed before he realized that the picture that memory, by some strange caprice, had thrust before his eyes was Saint Sebastian as Mantegna had depicted him.

Toward afternoon a bit of color appeared in the priest's cheeks, and he fell into a calm and refreshing sleep. But soon he began to be delirious. He raised himself and tried to lean on his elbows but immediately fell back again on the pillows. He stammered incomprehensible words that finally turned into a prolonged groan and burst from time to time in short sobs. The worried doctor bent over him, but it was merely the somnolent reaction of a long period of unconsciousness that must have been full of bad dreams. Although he had no fever, the sick man sometimes seemed to be on fire. His face and neck and the chest exposed by his open shirt burned to the touch.

Padre Rocca's sleep had that wealth of content that only comes in moments of mortal illness or danger.

Although we know little of the essence of dreams, we know at least that they let us observe the past without those empty interludes, those clamorous or simply insignificant blank passages of the stream of time. So we often see reality compressed in an instantaneous flash, instead of the authentic, diluted version of the past that, no matter how dramatic at the moment, loses much of its drama with the passing of the years. For this reason, what we see in dreams sometimes seems more real than the actual events that we have seen with our open eyes assuring us of that tangible consistency which is altogether incomparable to the volatile substance of dreams. A dream extracts what is essential from the disordered chaos of life, and even if its unravelling takes only a few minutes on the clock of our existence, a dream gives such a larger sense of continuity, of consistency, of logical sequence, of clarity and precision; in short, of those characteristics which the world lacks, tottering as it does on the edge of nonsense and compared by the poet to a story told by an idiot, full of sound and fury. But in order that the secret of the great moment of contact between life and death will never be revealed, and so that no one may boast (even at the end or at the threat of the end) that he has been allowed to observe his own life from the other shore, he returns at daybreak from the world of dreams with his tongue torn out, as if returned from the slavery of an enemy jealous of his secrets. No one has ever succeeded in recounting his dream with precision. Awakening reduces the illusion of the dream to the level of the illusion of reality in the tale of the idiot, full of sound and fury. One returns with a disordered impression that is impossible to straighten out and explain; it vanishes like a puff of smoke, which can never regain its lost form. Once the dream is over, its richness, its logic, its clarity become the nothing after an explosion—mere fragments of an immaterial and surprising structure.

So it was with Padre Rocca. Much later, when he had regained his strength, he remembered his crisis in a calmer mind. And from the ruins of that dream he could exhume only a few relatively clear fragments. He was certain that there was an enormous range in the picture, yet he stood perplexed before it, like a man who has seen the whole picture in a flash for a moment but has only retained one or two isolated fragments of the whole—too casual and vaguely related to form the basis of a total reconstruction.

Padre Rocca saw Immacolata just as she had been that day, but somehow changed. It was that afternoon when solitude had clutched his throat (for only solitude, and not the hunger of the body he had long since dominated, stole his reason and demanded that simple contact with life and with the world) and had driven him to that madness whose sinful fruit lay at the foot of Monte della Madonna dei Marini. In reality he had knelt before Immacolata and begged her consent, trembling with emotion, certainly ludicrous in his stammering, his heart flooded with self-hatred and hatred for her and all the cruel work of creation. Repulsed by Immacolata, he became enraged at the thought of his own humiliation and used violence. But all that appeared in a completely different way in the dream.

In the dream Immacolata was standing by the open window, and the rays of the sun caressed her bronze-colored hair. A sudden gust of wind blew through her thick tresses, and hundreds of golden glints seemed to fan out against the blue background of the sky. She did not look at him. She was looking up, with her hands joined in the hollow under her breast. The joy of life, as he had never before so fully sensed it, filled him with a sense of sweet impotence. It seemed, if he remembered correctly, that there was no one on the island but Immacolata and himself. He heard a strange song without words, as if all the colors of the gulf had been transformed into glass bubbles of different tones and were struck against each other in all directions by an invisible hand. He approached her, fell to his knees, and threw his arms about her waist, but she fell over a precipice like a statue toppled from a high rock, screaming *aiuto, aiuto*! That scream was doubly linked to reality. It had broken from her lips that afternoon, and she had come to him with the same cry the evening of that July day when Sebastiano, after hearing her confession, had leapt at her by the Certosa wall with his eyes full of blood, only to cover them a minute later with outstretched fingers, screaming in pain.

"You have to get away from here," Dr. Sacerdote said when the sick man finally awoke, opened his eyes with difficulty, and asked for water. "You must ask for a transfer."

The priest smiled melancholically. "What else do I have in life besides my habits?" he replied.

It was the priest's friend who, two months later, left the island forever.

IX

Thus, although it was the middle of May 1950, there still were not many tourists. Once a day when the boat came from Naples, the funicular, like a trawl, would haul a group of people up from the harbor below and unload them in the square. They would stop for a moment among the tables of the only café, take a quick glance around at the people, look up at the clock tower as if they wanted to remember the precise hour of their arrival, and then disappear down the narrow streets and paths into the depths of the island.

The weather was sunny and cool. Between late afternoon and dusk, as the sun withdrew behind the cover of Monte del Sole, the people around the tables of the café slowly emerged from the shadow of their reveries and looked around the square for the still-warm patches of sunset luster. In the morning some of the tourists from the northern countries went down to the sea, but even they returned to the town right after their swim and waited patiently, not hurrying the season.

Spring came late that year. It had been hot, almost scorching, in January and February, and then the winter rains fell. In March and April the sky hid behind low clouds, the air turned sooty like the glass of a kerosene lamp, and a fire burned on the hearth of more than one house on the island. The sea, the color of bluing in dirty soapsuds, pounded monotonously against the rocky shore. Occasionally the hazy outlines of the mainland and the neighboring islands were visible.

At the beginning of May a clear, dry wind brought the island's overdue spring. The sea calmed; lightly wrinkled in the morning, splashed with sun at noon, it seemed to paste translucent flakes of blue-green along the shore. The vegetation of gardens and vineyards, of pine woods and fruit trees glowed against the tawny yellow background of rocky cliffs and naked mountain ridges. All the magic of the water, the stone, and the secret filters of the sky oozing in from the outside came to life again in the island's grottoes—the Green Grotto, the Azure Grotto, the Violet Grotto. And the church bells chimed as if they were alloyed of glass and metal.

In the morning concert of the bells, the little bell on Monte della Madonna dei Marini sounded weakest of all. There was a pause after the first strong knell, broken by the dying heartbeats of iron on bronze; they were strung out like broken pearls, smaller and ever quieter, until they melted in their own echoes. Then a few more knells, but violent and rapid as if the bell-ringer hoped to overcome his fatigue with sheer obstinacy, like a traveler on the last stretch of road before the peak. Again a chaotic sequence of broken sounds and echoes filled the air, bouncing off each other, suffocating, going off in all directions, and gradually vanishing in the commotion of a new day and in the cries of the fishermen. There was one final knell, deep, prolonged, and abruptly cut off. The silence that followed was so long that it seemed that the bell-ringer must still be hanging onto the rope.

Listening to the music of the bell in the church on Monte della Madonna dei Marini, it seemed as if a human heart and not one of iron was talking about itself to the island. In the village at the foot of the mountain, people shrugged their shoulders: "Poor Padre Rocca, he's sick. He's growing old."

And, in fact, the priest had aged greatly in those last six years; he submitted to his illness without a struggle. His short figure was bent rather than hunched. He performed the mass on quivering, swollen legs, and when he raised his arms in the gesture of the offertory, his legs trembled like the flames of the candles on the altar. He still went down to the village under his own power to minister to the dead and dying, seldom as that was; but he always required two persons to help him back up the mountain.

Besides this, his solitude had been put to a new test for more than six months. Although Sebastiano had not been very well received when he first came to Monte della Madonna dei Marini, the priest had become so used to him (particularly after Dr. Sacerdote's departure) that whenever the mason failed to appear at morning mass, the priest of the Madonna of Seafarers felt rather like an abandoned orphan. Such is the secret bond that links human destinies: in solitude, the rope that chokes the throat becomes a life belt. Even the shadow of guilt slowly vanishes and at the end disappears; a hand with blood flowing in its veins finds nothing in the glow of the sun but its own shadow. After mass Sebastiano would rest on the steps of the church. Padre Rocca would sit down beside him and tell him what he had never been able to confide to any human ear or even to the silence of the tomb—perhaps because Sebastiano was neither one nor the other, and at the same time both. Perhaps the priest had long felt the need of confession. And as he retreated fearfully from the world, he may have found a desperate courage in the presence of a man whose only link to the world was his infirmity and spiritless existence. Whether it was right or wrong, the priest was greatly relieved to find a confidant in the man who was the principal subject of his sad story.

But as hard as he tried, he could not or would not reveal the whole truth even to his deaf confidant. Who, after all, can tell the whole truth about himself? We are forsaken like children lost in the woods. When you stand before me and look at me, what do you know of my sufferings and what do I know of yours? And if I fell at your feet and cried and told you, would you know any more about me than you know about hell when they say it is hot and sets one shivering? No, Padre Rocca could find no words to express his deeply hidden suffering other than those, inept and shameful, that blamed all his error and sorrow on solitude. Although he was an articulate man, he was as mute as his listener. And Sebastiano? He could not find a fictitious refuge from his sorrow in words. Perhaps he understood nothing or too little of it; he did not, luckily for him, have to look blindly into its cold eyes. Often at the most touching moment of the priest's monologue, Sebastiano would unexpectedly get up and, as if he were altogether unaware of the speaker's presence, he would drag his weary legs toward the path that led to the lower part of the island.

Sebastiano had stopped going to Monte della Madonna dei Marini at the beginning of the preceding November. One rainy morning at dawn the youngest monk at the Certosa, Fra Giacomo, found Sebastiano lying motionless in a ditch at the foot of the wall behind the Prior's Garden, near the edge of the plateau over the sea—under that same piece of wall which Sebastiano had left unrestored years before and which (like a perennial memento of the event) had remained gray-green like the patina of the rocks, in marked contrast with the white of the rest of the girdle of the Certosa. Who knows if the young monk—only recently transferred to the island from the monastery of Altamura, in Apulia, to take the place of a dead companion—knew the story of the Certosa well enough to wonder for a moment, as he looked at the man lying face down (it could have been a dead man wrapped in rags), if the seventeenth-century invaders of that terrified fortress had not looked like that, when the column of the plague-ridden reached the last bastion of the Prior's Garden. But the Certosa was free of its former faintheartedness, and only wanted to redeem itself and extirpate the past shame forever, so a moment after he was discovered, Sebastiano found himself being carried by all four brothers toward the *Chiostro Piccolo.* One of the monks had lifted Sebastiano's body before, on July 25, 1933.

It was an acute inflammation of the lungs, a serious threat to an organism so enfeebled by wandering; and the struggle to drive the specter of death from the little cell where the vagabond had been laid lasted several weeks. The day before Christmas Eve the convalescent crossed the threshold of his enforced confinement and, meeting no obstacles, headed slowly for the *Chiostro Grande*. He seemed to want to leave the Certosa, and Fra Giacomo even carried the sailcloth bag, hurriedly filled with provisions, as far as the gate. An unexpected thing happened: after making a circuit of the arcades of the portico, lightly touching the columns with his right hand as if they were the strings of a stone harp, Sebastiano returned to his cell by the same path he had taken when he came into the large courtyard of the monastery.

Neither the next day nor any day following did Sebastiano leave the Certosa. Its four inhabitants glowed with a silent joy. In the eyes of the whole island, the man who had driven his naked, scarred feet back and forth across the island for sixteen years, as if he could no longer find a place for himself in the rude and sun-scorched soil of his native land, had finally found a spot where he could rest. Had Sebastiano's aimless wandering finally exhausted and undone him? Had two months of illness rooted out his desire to live in the roads and paths of the little world surrounded on all sides by the sea? No one expected an answer to these questions, and who could answer them except the man who had settled into a new existence in the Certosa, and his lips were firmly sealed. But similarities again suggested themselves, because, like children lost in the woods, we seek in comparison a sense of continuity and existence, like signs carved in the bark of trees by the hand of our predecessors. Once before, the Certosa had received a benefactor into its hands, so that he might meet death within the walls that, in gratitude for the birth of his first heir, he had constructed to the greater glory of Heaven among the generations to come. Although it had been no fault of his own, Sebastiano had been unable to complete the restoration of the Certosa walls. Could one be sure that it was not for this reason (as the inhabitants of the island believed) that his first offspring, born out of wedlock, now lay in the little cemetery at the foot of Monte della Madonna dei Marini? It was up to the Certosa to balance the accounts of its erstwhile restorer; Sebastiano had not managed by himself to repay Providence for that miserable crumb of happiness which had been his on this earth. And so, contrary to the hopes and expectations of the monks, the old note of aversion again marked the island's relations with the Certosa.

The Certosa acquired a new penitent. What sins could he have to atone for, Sebastiano, who had exchanged a vagabond's mat for a monastery cell and a cloak of rags for the habit of a penitent? Why renounce his vagabond liberty and submit to the severe code of contrition? No one knew (and who could have known?) that, before pain ripped a scream from the mason's throat that hot afternoon, the life of the pregnant woman standing before him had hung for a moment by a thread. Even the medieval chroniclers did not know in what circumstances and by whose hand the wife of the prince-secretary of Joan of Anjou had died shortly before the success of the plot against the throne.

Sebastiano did not replace his ragged garments with an expiatory habit, but with the tunic of the monastery. He donned the habit, in conformity with local usage (although it is dying out), of the *monaco di casa*, whereby lay people who do not take monastic orders can live in their own homes withdrawn from worldly interests. Actually Sebastiano had been much more of a monk when he wandered about the island with the patient step of a pilgrim than he was after he found home and refuge within the Certosa. Although no one urged him or obliged him to do so, he worked in the Prior's Garden in the morning. And by spring it already seemed that the Garden, grown wild except for the little vineyard by the wall, had by the grace of God regained part of its former magnificence. One could rack one's brain to figure out how Sebastiano managed to work with such precision. He must have been able to see something, because no sooner had he pulled up the weeds than he brought forth a lawn so symmetrical that a gardener stringing lines on pegs would have been proud of it. The monks were even more astonished when he began helping Fra Giacomo in his workshop in the evenings.

Before entering the monastery of Altamura, Fra Giacomo (who came from Benevento) had done a bit of carving and after the war had won a certain renown for a wood reproduction of the famous bronze doors of the cathedral in his hometown, which were almost completely destroyed in a bombing in 1943. When he arrived on the island, not only did he immediately appreciate the beauty of what, besides the Roman excavations, was its principal treasure, the *Pietà dell' Isola*, but he also took it into his head to make it one of the sources of income of the impoverished Certosa. Counting on the tourist trade, Fra Giacomo began to copy the work of the anonymous Sienese master in the form of little altars to be sold as souvenirs of the island. When he had been brought to the workshop by the young monk, Sebastiano sand-papered the sculptures before they were painted: the work required only a normal sense of touch. Very soon, however, Sebastiano was reaching for the chisel, and with astounding precision he corrected Fra Giacomo's hurried work. While he worked he held his head in the position in which he used to look for the sun in the sky. It was useless to wonder whether he saw something through the crack in the corner of the right eye, or whether it was necessary to see at all with those hands, every nerve of which had remembered since childhood the forms of the *Pietà dell'Isola*. In May Sebastiano fell ill again. This time the cause of the suffering was not clear, and it was feared that he would die. He lay in his cell with his face to the wall, he refused food because he had obvious difficulty in swallowing, he slept continuously, and he only awoke to reach into the shadows for a cup of camomile or punch on the little trunk by his bed. As he slept, there was a hoarse rattle in his throat in which only the monk who had witnessed the accident seventeen years before detected a familiar note. Sometimes during his sleep he would bend his arms and cover his cheeks, forehead, and eyes as if he were shielding them, or as if he were defending himself from some menacing phantom.

The news of the danger that threatened his life quickly spread throughout the island. Although they had known during the preceding illness of his lungs that the chances of saving him hung in a delicate balance, it was only now that the islanders wondered what they would do without him. He had become as inseparable a part of the island as the slopes of the rocks, the naked crests of the mountains, the colored grottoes, the Madonna dei Marini with her arms raised on high, the black cross that commemorated the death of the nine fishermen, and the lighthouse on Monte del Faro. The gate of the Certosa was open all day, and people were continually gathering to talk in whispers (a superfluous courtesy, alas) as they waited for some news from the monks who took turns at the bedside of the mortally tired pilgrim. Baskets of fruit, fish, fresh bread, and wine were brought from the farthest villages. Since Sebastiano had scarcely touched food in his waking moments, there was something about it all that suggested a pagan sacrifice to the hesitant and pensive god that slowly weighed the poor man's fate in his hands. Never had such close bonds of cordial intimacy linked the island and the Certosa as in the second half of May 1950, dispersing the shadows of the ancient and the recent past. Two or three times a day Immacolata came up from the bar in the square. Toward the end of the month the boy who served at the mass in the church of the Madonna dei Marini led Padre Rocca down on muleback. Intrigued by the continual traffic to the Certosa, the first tourists on the island entered the gates of the Certosa. "Our Sebastiano is dying," they were informed in a tone that precluded the thought that someone might not know who the dying man was.

In the end life tipped the balance. June came, the weather suddenly turned warmer, and the season began in earnest, attracting hundreds of new arrivals every day, foreigners and Italians. It was then that Sebastiano raised himself on his elbows and indicated that he wanted to sit up. A bowl of soup was brought to him at once. The courtyard of the monastery resounded with loud shouts. A couple of hours later the whole island—from Monte della Madonna dei Marini to Monte del Faro, from the harbor to Capo Scogliera —had heard the joyous news. The island had no idea for what purpose the Supreme Judge had destined him, when, at the end of June, Sebastiano returned to work in the Prior's Garden and in Fra Giacomo's workshop.

X

Although summer arrived late, it was hotter than it had ever been. The older people on the island could not remember a hotter summer.

Early in the morning it seemed as if the sun had already reached its zenith at double or triple speed. Like an unchecked fire, drawn from ignited tinder to an enormous pile of hay so dry that it crumbled between the fingers, the heat enveloped the island in one long hot breath. The tourists who followed the winding paths down to the sea were careful not to touch the rocks in the narrow passes, they were so hot. The blue of the sky took on a shading of ashen color, and a solar fog in the air veiled the horizon with white smoke, so that at most a mile or so of the water surrounding the island was visible. Naked bodies throbbed in every corner of the island, even on the unfrequented dunes of Capo Scogliera; the water along the shore bubbled as it does when nets full of fish are hauled up. The gulls hung over the water in tired flight. The daily pauses to irrigate the fields and vineyards were always briefer. The heat killed the perfumes of the island, absorbing everything in the sharp, brackish smell of algae putrefying on the beaches. Only toward nightfall the sweet-sour perfume of the fruit trees and the flowers filled the air. And farther up, toward the peaks of the highlands, waves of mint and sage mingled in the air. After only a couple of hours, the initials that tourists carved in the cactus leaves and on the agaves looked as if they had been impressed with iron bands heated in coals. Colors, white and green in particular, no longer belonged to objects but were simply the abstract intensity of the essence of color. The same was true of the forms of objects. The houses bunched together on the slopes and the palms strung across the rocky terrain looked like flat designs on glass that owe the illusion of solidity and a third dimension only to the play of the rays of the sun.

One could best get an idea of the heat of the island when people could no longer hold their heads up— in the hours of siesta. From one to four, and sometimes even till five, life stopped. In the sultry and heavy silence every hammer blow, every human voice or click of wooden sandals had in its sound and echo something viscous and slow. In the emptiness, whitened to incandescence, every solitary walker hesitated with a drunken step in the bondage of his own dark shadow.

The sweltering heat did not disappear at night, but the horizon cleared. The solar fog evaporated shortly before sunset. As the sun began to descend behind the nearby island and shot out its last sanguine beams, all along the line that separated sky and sea the horizon seemed to burst into flames that consumed the opaque white veil. Red and pink bands, in various shades that gradually darkened at the edges as if they were trimmed with Spanish lace, marked the limits of vision, and oblong clouds, whose existence no one would have suspected in those hot and windless days, sprang into sight. Not the slightest breeze blew from the sea. But the air gradually became more transparent; and scarcely had the last strip of sky darkened after sunset than Naples, invisible by day, appeared covered with a network of little lights.

Sunset was the sign of truce. In the little streets near the square, and in the square itself, the people came together in turbulent, uneasy crowds. There was something in the evening strolls that suggested the prudent moderation and hesitancy of a convalescent's steps. Tents rose on the beaches, and motionless groups of tourists stood out on those points from which guides insist one must admire the beauty of the island, their glances caressing the silvery water that sweetly and lazily brushed against the rocks.

Only the late hours disbanded and scattered that crowd looking for a breath of lighter air. When twelve strokes rang from the clock tower, the silence of the island deepened as it did during the siesta. The air remained hot with the vapor of the daylong heat but acquired a silken delicacy toward dawn. During the full moon, until long after midnight, a strange, phosphorescent luminosity pervaded the island and gave everything prodigiously expressive outlines, as if they were engraved in dark glass. To someone observing this panorama from a ship, it would have seemed that the sea, suffused with moonlight, did not separate the island from the surrounding islands and from the mainland, but that it preserved the island from the fate of the rest of the world submerged in darkness— solitary and asleep, looking like a kneeling hooded monk with his head bent forward to the earth.

July and August passed. In September there was still no indication that summer had passed its apogee and that nature would begin to fold up the outspread fan of sun, shortening the days and freshening the wind.

XI

Because the air was clear at night, the fireworks of the Piedigrotta festival and the lights of the city of Naples were visible during the first half of September.

From sunset till two in the morning the entire Neapolitan shore glowed, and its reflection rose above the horizon in a thin, multicolored skein. At first the fireworks were set off timidly and sporadically in anticipation of the culminating moment of the *festa*: they exploded high in the sky like flowers that had suddenly bloomed, and then poured out purple and blue streams that were extinguished halfway down over the ashen sea front.

Among the many pairs of eyes on the island that watched the distant reflections of the lights of the Neapolitan festival, one pair stared with unusual persistence. Early in the evening Fra Giacomo had stolen out of the Certosa and climbed the pine-and-olive-covered hill that blocked the Certosa from the Naples side of the island. He sat leaning his head against a tree trunk with his face toward the mainland city. Not even the sound of midnight from the clock tower in the square moved him. He lost all sense of time and, although night had long since darkened all the illuminations, he remained in a kind of torpor until dawn, when the morning chill aroused him.

It is not easy to say what it is that awakens the inexpressible reveries and nostalgia that slowly rise within the soul like birds in flight: a fragment of landscape, a single lighted window in a darkened house front, a glimmer on a distant shore, the smell of the earth, a heavy rain, or the murmur of the wind. Such thoughts seem to have their source in something concrete, yet they elude the tongue and never show themselves in full light; they slip through fingers too clumsy to catch and hold them. They seem to evoke the sensation of a continuous but vain approach to something unattainable—to the very root of consciousness, overgrown with sterile and emotionless years—

as if they sprang forth in those regions (near the dreams of delirium perhaps) where everything is somehow known but condemned to indistinct existence. And examined in detail they still do not reveal all of their secret nature, yet sometimes they can suddenly drive a man to an act that no one can understand.

Fra Giacomo had been on the island less than a year. And in that time he had rarely thought of the monastery of Altamura in the sad dead plain of Apulia, with its countless naked hills sinking into lime bogs, its dwarf olives clinging to the reluctant earth like the roots of some enormous tree that has not been altogether uprooted, and its peasants barely distinguishable from monks in their black and dark-brown cloaks. For Fra Giacomo the Certosa had been a change for the better, for he had not sought in the monk's tunic the severity and poverty that strengthen faith, but merely oblivion from war; and where besides the island, barely grazed by the war, would it have been easier to forget the churches and homes in flame, the burned corpses of one's closest relatives, children dismembered by the exploding bombs, a masterpiece of art reduced to dust? Having abandoned the world as he had seen it in his youth, he found the grace of a memory without pain among the white walls of the Certosa and the beauties of the island.

Perhaps the world had returned to him now in the lights of the Neapolitan festival that brightened the mainland shore with a strip of colored light, or in the murmur of the sea's converse with the moon, or in the hot, sweet air that wound around the leaves of the olive and the needles of the pine. Fra Giacomo closed his eyes, and from his childhood the sounds of those holidays celebrated everywhere in Campania, with their songs alternately mournful and gay and the sound of broken glass and fireworks crackling in the air, came back to him. But it was not this that plumbed the source of his nostalgia and vague longing. Not this, but a feeling to which he had vainly struggled to attach a name or face, a feeling that embraced everything around him but lingered nowhere. When he folded his hands on his knees he seemed to touch one of the statuettes that he had carved in the Certosa and to read its forms with the fingers of a blind man. He mused: since the world has been, someone has always fallen only to be lifted in arms of mercy; since the beginning, the sea has patiently washed away the blood of the dead, the moon has imperturbably illuminated the houses of the living deep in sleep, while the sunlashed island rests and refreshes itself in the arms of the night. How to repel that world and withdraw from it forever?

The last night of the Neapolitan *festa* there was a veritable storm of fireworks. They rose suddenly on all sides like a confused antiaircraft barrage, they burst open at the same altitude and traced ever-new patterns on the vaults of heaven—flowers, then a rain of incandescent ash, scattered comets, then necklaces and rings, and gushing fountains. No corner of the sky was empty, and the whole gulf shook with the cannonade. Delirium gripped the mainland city: hardly had one wave of shouts subsided when another began. The sea sparkled like a mirror reflecting countless chandeliers. The stars had all been blown away, who knows where, and the moon shone through a crack in the luminous clouds no brighter than a modest street lamp. The Castel dell'Ovo was submerged in a flood of fireworks: the ancient fortress of the Normans and Angevins glowed brilliantly for a moment and then waved a black banner of smoke. Perhaps the island remembered not only the recent war but also the funeral signs of the plague year.

It was only a few days till September 19 and the festival of the *Pietà dell'Isola*, which was to fall on a Thursday that year. That Wednesday after sunset, unbeknown to his three fellow monks at the Certosa, Fra Giacomo boarded the *vaporetto* to the mainland that brought provisions every month to the lighthouse at the foot of Monte del Faro. He did not regret that step which no one except himself—on the island nor in Benevento, nor in the monastery of Altamura—could have understood. He felt some regret as the island swiftly receded against the clear gray sky. And he felt regret for the one person on the island to whom he had felt close, the man whose friendship he could never repay with even a single miserable word. If the young monk had only known what his flight would mean to the vagabond guest of the Certosa!

XII

Fra Giacomo was missed at the Certosa the next morning at dawn. One of the brothers knocked at the door of his cell after matins; there was no answer. Inside, the folded bed and the empty shelf left no room for doubt.

In the chapel the three remaining monks looked at each other, and then at the sculpture of the *Pietà dell'Isola* by the side altar. Together they managed to lift the sculpture onto the litter and drag it—setting it down every few steps and changing positions at the front handles—as far as the portico of the *Chiostro Grande*. The gate of the Certosa was still closed. Again day had broken with a bright sun and without wind, but a wave of fresher air seemed to be coming toward the island from the sea: nature itself was coming to the *festa* that marked the decline of summer and the end of the season. Although the procession never left the Certosa before ten, when the last gong of the clock tower was answered by the two bells of the church in the square, the sound of preparations could already be heard beyond the walls: thin voices of children, shouts of men and women, fragments of hymns that were to be sung in procession by choirs of children. Someone fired off two trial fireworks: like pennons of lamb's wool they hung suspended in the brilliant blue of the sky.

Shortly before the designated time the three monks bearing the statue emerged from the portico into the open courtyard near the gate. Between the dark tunics and the milky glow of the morning light, the sun sank into the black of the Madonna's kerchief and sparkled over her golden tresses. The garment that covered the bent figure was as blue as the sea at night. On the rigid ashen figure of the Son, the rays of the sun seemed to resculpture the curling hair and the knotted beard, the spikes of the crown of thorns, the sharp cheekbones, and the tight cleft of the mouth. Perhaps God Himself wished to end the old tradition and unite the island and the Certosa in a supremely simple gesture of mutual help and humility in the presence of that sculptured representation of pain and mercy? Perhaps He had already chosen the man behind the walls to take the place of the fugitive and to open the way to a final reconciliation.

Just then Sebastiano made his appearance at the end of the arcade that led to the Prior's Garden. He set his pails down, closed the door behind him, and, picking up the pails again, walked to the well in the center of the courtyard. After two illnesses he was thinner and weaker than ever. His step acknowledged a decay of the body for which there is no medicine. Sebastiano let the bucket on the chain all the way down; it cost him an obvious effort to wind the chain back, and several times he stopped to hold the handle for a moment in his bony hand. He drank deeply and immersed his head in the bucket. Then he filled the pails and sat down on the edge of the well, his wet face turned toward the sun. The three monks exchanged a glance, and one of them went to the well. Sebastiano made no objections to the monks' proposal. At the sound of the church bells the gate was opened, and the *Pietà* emerged on the shoulders of four bearers.

Sebastiano walked in front on the right so that anyone could see at once that the Certosa had no intention of hiding the sad truth, and so that Sebastiano would carry less weight as the bearers walked along. The crowd opened wide and stopped in silence. "Where is Fra Giacomo?" someone shouted, then cut himself short as if he were ashamed of his own voice. The children, dressed in white, unaware of what had happened, decked the statue with flowers, confetti, and colored paper streamers; the little girls timidly intoned the first hymn. But the funereal silence of the older people broke the usual order of the procession. Slowly, with four pairs of sandals shuffling, the procession moved forward as the stunned crowd looked on. Even the sound of the bells seemed alarmed, their solitary tolling unaccompanied by cheering voices. Above hundreds of heads the Madonna turned her serene but suffering glance not toward the Son but toward the neck with the knot of hair. As the procession went downhill, the head of the Redeemer hung so near the bent head of the bearer on the right that they could have touched at any moment. The procession stopped before the steps that led up to the square and the followers reassembled behind it.

It was obvious by now that Sebastiano was bearing a weight beyond his powers. His feet, which had known every inch of the island for years, stiffened for a moment in mid-step and trembled lightly in the air as if searching for a level spot on the ground. His knees trembled, and the veins in his calves rose and swelled. He struggled to breathe, with a hoarse and asthmatic wheezing; sweat rolled down his forehead and temples, and, catching the bits of confetti stuck to his cheeks, bore them down to his beard; he clawed his fingers into the coarse shaft of wood. But in his face, under the contracted membranes and particularly in the crack in his right eye, the feverish labor of thought seemed to be reawakening from a long torpor; as if he remembered something, as if every step took him farther back into time, as if he were traversing an enormous distance with those cautious steps, as if he were recognizing piece by piece the burden he was bearing—and in the September sun Sebastiano did not bleed, he liquefied.

At the foot of the stairs, when the procession stopped to catch its breath, the people nearest the front pair of bearers saw that the blind man's lids had opened slightly and that tears were flowing down his cheeks.

As the procession climbed the stairs, most of the weight of the sculpture was borne by the two bearers in the rear, but Sebastiano suddenly betrayed signs of distress. Either he had lost his grip on the pole on his shoulder, or his feet had lost their almost dance-like rhythm and touched the steps too soon. In any case, something like panic gripped him and seemed to pull him forward as a horse drags forward with an over-

loaded cart on a slippery road. At one point the *Pietà
dell'Isola* tilted perilously to one side, and a murmur
of horror rose from the crowd. Sebastiano straightened
up, readjusted the pole on his shoulder, and moved
forward with a calmer step. His face was as wet as it
had been when he sat on the well and looked up at the
sun.

Farther along, the road was straighter and smoother.
But that piece seemed to give him more difficulty than
the stairs. The previous exertion must have brought
him to the limit of his endurance, for in the heavy
and sometimes wavering movements of his body there
was more of a mechanical trance than a muscular
effort. The sun shone with greater force. The crowd
was altogether silent, and the only sound beside the
bells was the shuffle of feet behind the statue. The procession reached a point where the road narrowed.
Lasciate passare, "Let us pass," the monk in front
cried vainly at those who stood on both sides. Jostled
by someone, Sebastiano fell abruptly to one side. His
knees buckled and his feet spun out of his sandals,
as if he wanted to kneel. *Aiutatelo*, "Help him," a
woman cried. It was impossible to recognize whose
voice it was in the noise.

But the whole scene lasted only a few seconds. Sebastiano straightened himself again and took the next
step with confidence. The procession was nearing the
second ramp of stairs, beyond which the road arched
between the little houses of the town and led easily into
the square.

XIII

Padre Rocca suffered the first seizure of choking
and the typical attack of fear that accompanies it
when he knelt at the altar after mass and could not

rise. The boy who served at mass grabbed the priest's elbow with both hands. Padre Rocca struggled to his feet, and glanced around the nave as he went into the sacristy. Ten or fifteen people had come to mass from the village at the foot of Monte della Madonna dei Marini before going to the *festa* of the *Pietà dell'Isola*. Padre Rocca would have given much if someone had stayed behind at least through the afternoon. Solitude threw him into a particular panic in such moments and disturbed the clarity of his mind. What frightened him most was the idea that God was ready to let him die alone. Returning to the parish house he saw the heads of the departing communicants at a bend in the road. He patted the boy's head and pushed him in the direction of people who were going away.

In his room Padre Rocca felt weak and choked again, but he did not have the courage to lie down. He was afraid of getting drowsy and exposing his sick heart to a blow in his sleep, without ever noticing the aggressor's approach or attack; there were hope and help if only he remained awake. So he walked around the room like a caged animal, stopping to look at the postcards on the walls and out the window at the deserted courtyard of the church. He stopped before the little black crucifix and cracked the knuckles of his locked fingers or closed his eyes and pressed his fingers to his lips in a rapid prayer: "Dear God, I ask very little: Thy will be done, but don't let me die alone." He decided to go out to the belvedere near the statue of the Madonna of Seafarers but then recoiled in terror from the idea. He realized that from the edge of the high rock wall he would see the immense deserted world and the motionless sea. And the waves beating in the grottoes at the foot of the mountain would surge in his brain.

He all but ran from the parish house, and only beyond the bend in the road, where he almost slipped, did he realize that he was headed down toward the village.

With his feet still gripping the ground, he leaned back, half lying against the slope of the hill and turned his head so as not to look down. His heart seemed to be tearing itself from his chest, and then it would contract as if it were being squeezed, while he desperately gasped for air. Again he murmured his prayer, "Dear God . . . ," each time emphasizing the word "alone." Even if he had to drag himself on all fours he felt that he must reach the village. He had never felt such terror; he almost leapt over the precipice. But the impulse passed in a moment. He did not expect that anyone in the village could help him. But the sun, the sun, *il sole*! He burned with the desire to see human faces around him.

When he had regained his strength and his calm, he began the descent very cautiously and very slowly. Oh, if someone would see him! He instinctively cupped his hands under his heart and bent over almost to the ground, as if he were holding a precious and fragile object that, at the slightest jar, would fall from his hands and shatter into tiny pieces. But it was unlikely that anyone would see him before he reached the village. The path was deserted except for the lizards basking in the sun, who fled before him and disappeared with a rapid swish into the holly that bordered the path. There were no trees, and the cracked leaves of the agave and cactus that seemed glued to the rock offered no shade at all.

He reached the point where a crevice opened up and the path turned for about a hundred yards along the back of the hill that blocked the sea view from both sides of the island—far away to the right, almost straight off to the left. Two persons could barely walk abreast at this point in the path, and every time Padre Rocca had been accompanied from the village, one of his escorts had had to let go of his arm and walk behind. When the priest went down to the village alone, it was only here that he slowed his pace and avoided looking to the left. Now he stood as if rooted to the ground and was afraid to move. Yet only a few minutes before he had been ready to throw himself over the precipice! How many faces the hidden fear of a sick heart shows!

From where he stood one could see the little road below that led along the cemetery wall: it seemed farther and more unattainable than ever. At most he was half a mile from the little bench set up for tourists at the halfway point from the peak. He remembered that winter evening almost seven years before when he had found relief in the sight of a friend sitting on that bench.

After Dr. Sacerdote left the island, he sent the priest a picture postcard from Mantua twice a year, at Christmas and Easter, with a couple of lines of greetings and inquiries after his health. But Padre Rocca had never answered them, and in the end the thread that bound him to his past and his hometown was broken. The cards adorned one wall of the room in the parish house, making the discolored and worn reproduction of the *Pietà dell'Isola* on the opposite wall seem even lonelier. Thus his life passed, leaving traces no larger than the footprints left by a lost traveler in the sands of the desert. So little remained on Monte della Madonna dei Marini when the flood of the war subsided. Life, real life, was down there where, after the footpath turned off, the little road led past the cemetery to the village. In the course of thirty years, thousands of men and women had whispered through the confessional grating the story of a life he could never know, even though he had the power of condemning or absolving that life. Once he too had gone astray, and a low cross planted in the cemetery was the eternal marker. Nevertheless he absolved himself in the depths of his soul, like all those over whom the Madonna on the hill watched—because there was no other life. There was no other life beyond that from which he gave absolution and toward which he sinfully aspired. There had never been any sin other than this, that men are born, defend themselves from solitude, and fear death. "Dear God, forgive me, have mercy on Your lost servant!"

Padre Rocca's swollen legs constantly ached. He let himself fall onto a rock by the side of the road, looking first at the road up the hill and then at the steep slope of the rock wall. No, he could not decide. At the mere thought of that narrow pass he clenched his fists against his chest and felt his head spin. He looked toward the peak of the mount, with the fragile statue erect as a lightning rod. He could be back in no time if he had not had to pace his heart so cautiously. Now he regretted his impulse to flee the solitude of the parish house. He smiled bitterly as he remembered that he had sworn to reach the village, even on all fours. There was no chance of any inhabitant or tourist appearing before nightfall. Only Sebastiano might happen by at any hour. But Sebastiano had not emerged from the Certosa for several weeks.

Padre Rocca tried to master his terror and pull together the remains of his troubled mind. Was it possible, he wondered, that age and illness had so weakened him that after thirty years, knowing every inch of that pass, he was suddenly afraid of a few minutes of nervous apprehension. But Padre Rocca tried in vain. He looked down at the sea far below the escarpment and, as if he were seeing it for the first time, he marveled that never before had he had such a clear and distinct sense of its peril. He got up from the rock and tried to climb back up the mountain. He did not even get ten yards. Pallid and barely able to stand, the priest returned to the rock.

The sun rose higher now and shone directly in his face. He had left his hat in the parish house, so he put his sweaty handkerchief on his head and unbuttoned his cassock. At first he felt almost well in the lazy heat that enveloped him. But for fear of falling asleep, he kept his eyes open. He knew he could not endure the duel for long, but he did not surrender, and with lids only slightly lowered he stared with an obstinate courage at the yellow disk that throbbed so hard in its heart it seemed it must burst from the sky. Finally Padre Rocca gave in and clamped the handkerchief over his eyes. It was hard to keep his eyes open under the rosy glow.

When he awoke a sharp breeze burned his face. The torn handkerchief hung stiffly on the branches of a bush under the edge of the precipice. Some little time passed before he remembered where he was and why, and before he became aware of the sound of bells. *È uscita la Pietà dell'Isola*, he murmured, "The procession has begun." So it must have been ten o'clock; at least an hour had passed since he sat down. He listened again, and again he felt a strange sense of happiness: the echoes of the bells were like the tinkling of little glass spheres.

He did not know how much time had passed when he woke again. The air shook with explosions. The sound of the bells was almost lost in the din, but he could hear clearly, though smothered by the distance, the shout or song that rose from hundreds of human throats.

Padre Rocca got up and, as if enchanted or unconscious, staggered on without looking down at his feet.

XIV

Before the rockets shot off into the blue, and before the bells of the church in the square pealed a sweeter sound, shouts and songs rose from the crowd ahead as the procession reached the top of the second set of stairs and entered the last, almost flat stretch of road.

The road was wider now. After the exertion of the narrow crowded passage of the second set of stairs, Sebastiano felt a freer space around him and a flat surface under his feet. He seemed to have regained all his energy, and it appeared that he would reach his goal. But it only seemed so for a brief moment. At first he walked with the lightness and agility he had had when, still a young man, he wandered about the island in the first years after his accident. But he soon realized that he could no longer sustain himself, that he had nothing more to give in that last stretch before the end. Something in him had cracked and refused to obey him. Unable to get a new foothold, he swayed back and forth in one spot, as if he were standing on a sand dune. Suddenly, and everyone saw it, he began looking feverishly in all directions, as if he needed help, and his face was strangely excited. It was another four hundred yards at most to the church. *Aiutatelo*, "Help him!" Immacolata began to scream. This time her call was heard. Men's hands tore the pole from Sebastiano's convulsively clenched fists and set the litter with the statue on the ground. Freed of his burden, Sebastiano bent over, dropped his head to his chest, took a step forward, and fell heavily, like a tree sawn through that needs only a slight push to be toppled.

Immacolata rushed to him first. She turned him over on his back, and, kneeling over him, she carefully slid her shoulders under his neck and the upper part of his rigid body. He seemed dead or immersed in a deep sleep. The bells stopped ringing. The bright sun was nearing its zenith, and the people stood silent and motionless, while above the fruit trees and vineyards and gardens and the little white houses the blue sky rose like a bell of blue glass over the island and the sea in the distance. And it was hard to decide which of the two pairs of figures side by side on the ground was the sculpture of the Sienese master, and which more deserved to be called the *Pietà dell'Isola*! But only one came to life: Immacolata raised her head, the black kerchief fell from her gold-bronze hair, and her lament broke the silence.

No one who was there will ever forget Immacolata's lamentation. It was the lamentation of the south, penetrating in its primitive violence, half aggressive and half supplicating. It was not composed of words. Detached sounds, neither shouts nor sobs, formed a guttural litany. There were curses and humble prayers in that litany, guilt and redemption, despair and faith, the misery of the fall and the hope of resurrection, a curse on fate and submission to its judgment. Compressed into a few dense minutes, it evoked the sterile nights and vain sleep of seventeen years. It appealed to the sun, to the earth, to the sea, to the sky, to the crowd, to anything that could move mercy, anything that could grant a crumb of kindness to life. Its last penetrating note hung above the man she held in her arms, and its softer echo vanished in the direction of Monte della Madonna dei Marini. And, like a bird tired of flying, perhaps it fell into the cemetery at the foot of the mountain.

Those who remembered Immacolata right after the accident, when she cursed the Certosa, sensed that they were listening to the same lament they had heard then.

When she ran out of breath she let her head fall and looked into Sebastiano's face with dry eyes. She did not have to bend lower, to his lips, for one to see that she made a superhuman effort to rouse a spark of life. The seconds dragged by like hours. Sebastiano moved, and through the crack in his right eye he could see: not a quivering shadow broken into an infinite number of lesser shadows, but distinct colors and sharp outlines. For a moment he thought he was looking at the Madonna of Donnaregina, and he was amazed at the change. He did not see the medallion of the Infant on her breast, nor the angel to her right who defended her with his sword from the dragon; nor did he see the dark tomb of the Son on the other side. Then Sebastiano froze for a moment. A shiver ran through that body exhausted by the climb and by the weight of its burden, and that shiver seemed to free him from the last bonds that held him.

"Immacolata," he said. "Immacolata," he repeated, almost shouting. Only now was his real suffering to begin.

A single word rang out, *Miracolo*, a shout mixed with song. Fireworks were shot off in all directions, and flowers, paper stars and streamers, and a cloud of colored confetti filled the air. The rockets began to beat at the gates of heaven, and the bells, drowned by the exploding fireworks, rang out again. Then the monks stepped aside; other hands lifted the statue and carried it triumphantly to the church in the square, ending forever the island's aversion for the Certosa.

XV

That same evening the news passed from mouth to mouth on the island that at the very moment in which Sebastiano was resurrected (that word was used to describe the epilogue to the procession of the *Pietà dell'Isola* of September 19, 1950: *Quando è risorto il nostro Sebastiano*) the coagulated blood of the martyr of Pozzuoli liquefied in the Cathedral of Naples. But that was not exactly true—according to the Cathedral register for 1950, the miracle of San Gennaro had occurred even before the procession left the Certosa. But nothing has ever been able to persuade islanders that the two miracles were not simultaneous. The south is as addicted to miracles as lonely people are to dreams, and will not allow a single detail to detract from its miracles, even when they fail to withstand the simple checking of facts. For the people of the south find in miracles, in longing for them and waiting for them (like the lonely man in dreams), the hope that when reality is too cruel there can be deliverance from it.

The next day, however, a sad note disturbed the island's joy. Only a few tourists had gone up to Monte della Madonna dei Marini toward sunset on the day of the *festa*, and they had noticed nothing along the road. The next morning the boy who served mass for Padre Rocca did not find the priest of the Seafarers' Madonna in the church or in the parish house. As he was returning to the village he saw a handkerchief caught in a ginestra bush just over the edge of the precipice. He looked down and hurried on.

The remains of Padre Rocca, head split open and chest deeply gashed on a sharp point of rock, were found on a promontory about fifty yards above the level of the sea. It was a difficult job to drag the body to the narrow strip of beach where the boats came with the police and the fisherman who had been sent for help. It was impossible to establish the circumstances of death. Suicide was rejected, out of respect for the dead man's profession. But opinion wavered between sunstroke and a fainting spell brought on by his heart. The fact that the priest had left his hat behind in the parish house seemed to confirm the former verdict. But there was no reason why both possibilities could not be mentioned in the death certificate, and so they were. "He was sick, poor Padre Rocca," the inhabitants of the village at the foot of the mountain testified. "He had suddenly grown very old." Because he only came down in case of urgent need, and because it had been five months since the boy who served at mass had led him all the way to the Certosa, they decided that some vision or presentiment must have drawn him toward the procession of the *Pietà dell'Isola*. Everything, in those moments of joy and transport, was turned to the praise of the miracle.

Toward the end of September the season began to wane. The departing tourists watched the island diminish gradually in the distance, and in the transparent air of the last days of summer it seemed to break away from the background of sky, sea, and setting sun like the relief carving of a kneeling monk with his hooded head bent to the ground. Some of the tourists, as a memento of the scene of which they had been involuntary witnesses, carried away miniature carved altars, souvenirs of the island. As the boat neared the port of Naples the island disappeared behind the curtain of sunset, and the lighthouse on Monte del Faro began its ceaseless blinking.

THE TOWER

I

It was the summer of 1945, the Italian campaign had just ended, and I had been transferred from headquarters between Bologna and Ravenna to the Polish military mission in Milan. A few weeks after my transfer I applied for leave. I had decided to spend it somewhere in the quiet and solitude of the Piedmont countryside. By a stroke of luck, an Italian assigned to our mission had offered me the keys to a little house in the foothills of the Alps. A distant relative of his, a retired *ginnasio* teacher from Turin, had died there all alone just before the end of the war. The house had been unoccupied since the death of the old recluse.

The house stood on a slope that seemed to form the pedestal of the highest peak of the Mucrone in the vicinity, far above the highway from the central industrial town of the entire upland region. Although the house was on the slope, a wide dirt road, whose sharp curves were guarded by a low stone wall, linked it to the highway three kilometers away, on the outskirts of the nearby village.

The gravel-strewn drive in front of the house, shaded by several maples along an iron fence, led through a gate on one side into a small garden. At the end the old recluse had apparently only taken pains to see that the paths were not overgrown. On both sides of the driveway the wall altogether disappeared under a growth of ivy and wild grape. There were several rooms, all dark, that looked out on the slope, half overgrown with withered blackberry and bushes scorched by the sun. The easy access from the slope may have led the builder to put gratings in the windows, but even without these fixtures there was something of voluntary isolation about the slope that cut off the road from observation.

I took one of the front rooms on the ground floor for myself. The only traces of life in the whole house indicated the former owner's preference for that room too. Through a clearing between two maple trees there was a view of the Elvo valley, with its dark-green clumps of trees, bright patches of meadow, red splotches of roof tops clustered around church turrets, and the faded hoods of hillside castles far away on the horizon.

Although it was large and comfortable, the room had only one window, and it failed to dispel the gloom that hung there from daybreak till dusk or to dry up the open sores of dampness in the corners. The woodworm-eaten furniture, chairs, and a sofa from which the leather was peeling in long strips, a thicket of spiderwebs in the fireplace and on the shelves, and over a chest of drawers a mirror in a once-gilt frame that reflected one's face through a film of soot—it all seemed to harmonize perfectly with the four Piranesi etchings on the wall. Anyone who has seen his engravings knows that Piranesi had a keen predilection for ruins and that he managed to render them with a hint of flesh falling away from bones. In a scholarly essay about Piranesi's "Prisons," Aldous Huxley

writes that they express "the perfect pointlessness
... the staircases lead nowhere, the vaults support
nothing."

Above a table in the corner by the window hung a
much smaller etching by an unknown artist: against
a background of mountains stood a rectangular tower
girdled by a high wall and surmounted by a solid block
construction broken only by a few small window openings. It was not the artist's burin but an expression
of desperation and silent grief in the stone crown of
the tower, raised like a weakly clenched fist against
the black clumps of cloud, that made the landscape of
the drawing so morbid that, in comparison, Piranesi
seemed a bucolic poet of the ruins of antiquity.

On the table between two silver candlesticks lay
a small volume, so dirty and crumpled and greasy
with tallow that it was easy enough to guess it had
provided the last occupant's favorite reading for many
years. It was an Italian translation of François-Xavier
de Maistre's *Le Lépreux de la cité d'Aoste* printed in
Naples in 1828 in a limited edition of fifty numbered
copies. The translator left the book's motto, from
Thomson's *The Seasons*: "Winter," in the original
English:

> Ah little think the gay licentious proud,
> Whom pleasure, power, and affluence surround ...
> Ah little think they while they dance along ...
> How many pine ... How many drink the cup
> Of baleful grief ... How many shake
> With all their fiercer tortures of the mind.

II

The south side of the city of Aosta, De Maistre
recounts, was never densely populated. It presented,

instead, a view of pastures and cultivated fields reaching right up to the remains of a Roman wall and low stone fences that enclosed small kitchen gardens. Nevertheless, travelers often came by, drawn by two singular attractions. Near the southern gate of the city were the ruins of an ancient castle with a round tower, where, according to popular tradition, the jealous Count Renato of Challant imprisoned his wife, Duchess Maria of Braganza, and starved her to death; the tower is called *Bramafan*, the Cry of Hunger. Several hundred meters farther along the stone rubble of the Roman wall was a second tower, this one rectangular and constructed in part of marble; legend had christened it the Tower of Fright, *Torre dello Spavento*. It was believed to be haunted, and it was said that on dark nights a white lady appeared in the doorway holding a lamp in her hands.

The Tower of Fright was restored about 1782, and a wall over six feet high was built around it, because it was to be the refuge of a leper and his isolation from the world. The unfortunate man came from Oneglia, a small duchy on the Ligurian coast acquired by the House of Savoy in the fifteenth century. No one knows exactly how old the leper was when he was taken to the tower in which he was to die, but he was certainly not yet twenty. The Maurist hospital in Aosta assumed the responsibility of supplying him with food, and the local authorities provided him with a few pieces of furniture and garden tools. He saw no one except the man who brought him supplies from the hospital every week and the priest who occasionally brought the consolation of religion to the *Torre dello Spavento*.

During the Alpine campaign of 1797, fifteen years after the leper's arrival at the Tower of Fright, De

Maistre came to Aosta as an officer in the Sabaudian army. One day he was walking by the wall that girdled the tower and noticed a wicket gate standing open. His curiosity got the better of him and he walked in. He saw a modestly dressed man deep in thought leaning against a tree. Without turning his head at the sound of the creaking gate and the steps, the hermit called out in a sad voice, "Who are you, traveler, and what do you want?"

De Maistre explained that he was a foreigner and apologized for his intrusion; he had been attracted by the beauty of the garden. "Don't come near me, sir," the resident of the tower replied, stopping him with a wave of his hand. "Don't come near me. I am a leper."

De Maistre was quick to assure him, and with great warmth, that he had never in his life shunned the unfortunate. Turning his face toward his visitor, the leper replied: "Stay then, if, after seeing how I look, you can still find enough courage in your heart."

For a moment De Maistre was struck dumb by the sight of a face altogether disfigured by leprosy. "I'll stay gladly," he replied at last. "Perhaps my visit, begun in curiosity, may bring some relief to this house." ·

"Curiosity!" cried the leper. "I've never aroused any sentiment but pity. Relief! It's a great consolation just to see another human being and to hear a human voice. I had almost forgotten the sound."

The visitor was eager to know all about the man's dwelling. The leper put on a large hat, and the broad low brim almost entirely covered his face. He led his guest to a part of the sunlit garden where he bred rare flowers from the seeds of wild plants that grew on the Alpine slopes, trying with the secrets of the gardener's art to enhance their excellence and beauty. He encouraged his visitor to pick some of the most beautiful and quickly added that there was no danger. "I planted them," he explained, "I take pleasure in watering them and in admiring them, but I never touch them."

In this way he kept the flowers uncontaminated; otherwise he could never offer them to anyone. Occasionally the messenger from the hospital would pick some, sometimes children ran in from the streets for them. The children would rap on the gate; the leper would draw the bolt and run to the top of the tower in order not to frighten them or inadvertently harm them. From the window of the tower he would watch as they frolicked a while about the walks and then threw themselves on the flower beds. As they left they would turn at the gate, look up at him, and, making faces at each other, would break out laughing and call: *Buon giorno, Lebbroso!* "Good day, Leper." Those childish shouts were a source of strange delight to him.

He grew several varieties of fruit trees as well, and grape vines climbed to the top of the only fragment of Roman wall that remained in the precinct of the hermitage after the Tower of Fright had been sealed in its stone ring. The remains of that antique wall were so wide that steps had been carved in it and one could stroll along the top and see, beyond the enclosure, the far country, the plains, and the men in the fields, without being seen. This corner of the garden was the leper's favorite retreat. From here the town seemed like a desert. "You don't always find solitude in the heart of the forest or on the cliffs. The unhappy man is alone anywhere."

Now the leper seemed more inclined to talk about

himself. He had never known his parents; they had died when he was a child. He was left with only a sister, and she had died two years before. He had never had a friend. That was how God would have it. De Maistre asked him his name. "Ah," exclaimed the tenant of the tower, "my name is awful. It is *Leb-broso*! No one knows the surname I had at birth, nor the name I was given by christening. I am the Leper. That is my only claim on the attention of men. And may they never know that this earth bore me; may every memory of my existence perish forever."

His sister had lived with him in the Tower of Fright for five years. She was a leper too and shared his pain. He had tried to ease her suffering.

"What do you do with yourself in such absolute solitude?" asked De Maistre. "I must confess that the idea of eternal solitude frightens me; I can't even imagine it."

"He who loves his cell," replied the leper, "will find his peace there. *The Imitation of Christ* teaches us that. And I am beginning to understand the truth of those words of comfort."

In the summer the leper worked in his garden. In the winter he wove baskets and mats. He sewed his own clothes and prepared his own meals. The hours left after work he dedicated to prayer. Thus his years passed and when they had passed, they almost seemed short.

It is true that pain and discomfort make the days and nights seem long, but the years pass with the same speed. And in the lowest depths of misfortune there exists a satisfaction that the greater part of mankind never experiences, the simple pleasure of living and breathing. Sometimes the leper spent long summer hours without moving, delighting in the air around him and in the charms of nature. Then all his thoughts became vague and almost hazy. His sadness stiffened and fell to the bottom of his heart, but it caused no pain. His glance wandering over fields and cliffs brought him ever closer to inanimate objects. The leper loved them. Those things he saw day after day became the only companions of his existence.

Every night before going back into the tower he saluted the glaciers of Ruitorts, the dark forests on the slope of the St. Bernard, and the marvelous peaks that dominate the valley of the Rhème. Although the power of God may be as evident in the creation of an ant as in the creation of the universe, it was the magnificent view of the mountains that overpowered him. He could not look at those enormous masses covered with eternal snow without a sensation of religious stupefaction. But even in this expansive panorama he had his favorite spots: most of all the hermitage of Charvensod, where the last rays of the setting sun fell through groves and empty fields. At twilight he would glut his eyes on that scene, and it would set his mind at peace.

That hermitage had almost come to belong to him. Sometimes it seemed that he vaguely remembered having lived there in happier days and that the passage of time had merely dimmed his memory. What particularly moved him was the sight of the distant mountains fading at their peaks into the horizon. The thought of distance, like that of the future, awakened hope in him. His oppressed heart longed to believe that there existed an unknown land where he could finally taste all that happiness which he had only imagined in his nocturnal reveries. A secret instinct accomplished the rest: it transformed hope into possibility.

Had it not cost the leper a great effort of will, once having accepted his fate, not to let himself be overcome by despair, De Maistre wondered. No, the leper would be lying if he said he never felt anything other than resignation. He had not attained that utter self-abnegation which some anchorites achieve. He had not yet accomplished that supreme annihilation of all human feelings. He passed his life in constant battle, and even the help of religion was not always enough to check the course of his fantasies. Often his imagination dragged him, against his will, into an ocean of chimerical desires that spread before him a fantastic picture of an unknown world.

In vain had books taught him of human perversity and the disasters that cling like shadows to man's fate; his heart refused to believe what his eyes read. The lot of free men was that much more to be envied, the more miserable his own was. When the first spring wind blew through the Aosta valley, he felt its reviving warmth penetrate the marrow of his bones, and a lust for life violently overflowed in him, breaking all the dams that stood in its way. He would slip out secretly from his prison then and, drunk with space, wander about the neighboring fields. He avoided those same people that his heart so passionately yearned to meet. Hidden among the bushes on the hilltop like a wild beast, he embraced the entire town with his glance. From afar he would watch the inhabitants of Aosta, who barely knew he existed. He would stretch out his arms to them, crying out for his share of happiness. In his outpourings of rapture (he confessed it with shame) he sometimes embraced the trunks of trees in the woods, begging God to animate them and give him at least one friend. But the trees repulsed him with their cool bark and remained silent. Overcome with fatigue, almost at the end of his strength, he would return in the end to the tower and seek consolation in prayer.

Unhappy man, he suffered all the torments of body and soul together. And those of the body were not the worst. True, they became more painful every month, but then they gradually diminshed. When the moon first cut the sky with its thin sickle, the illness asserted itself with increased force. As the moon rounded into a disk, the malady lessened and seemed to change its nature: the skin on his body dried and turned white, and he felt almost no pain at all. The worst was not the pain in itself, but its eternal echo—insomnia.

"Ah! sleeplessness! sleeplessness!" the leper sighed. Unless you have known it yourself you cannot imagine how long and terrible the night is when you cannot close your eyes and when all there is before them is a future entirely barren of hope. No, no one could imagine it. The approach of dawn would find the leper so distraught that his thoughts were all confused, he no longer knew what was happening to him, and he fell victim to extraordinary hallucinations. He would imagine that some irresistible power was dragging him down to a bottomless pit. At other times black spots would weave back and forth before his eyes, increasing in size as they came toward him, and turn into mountains that finally crushed him. Sometimes clouds would emerge from the earth around him, and like swelling waves they threatened to swallow him up. When he tried to rise and free himself from these incubi, invisible chains seemed to bind him to his bed. No, they were not dreams. He always saw the same things, and the dread of these impressions exceeded the anguish of his body. But could not these horrible phantasms have been caused by a fever resulting from insomnia? The leper glanced hopefully at De Maistre. Ah, would that it were only fever! Would it please God that it were only fever! Till then the leper had always trembled at the thought that these were the first signs of madness.

De Maistre unconsciously moved nearer to the leper. "Aren't you afraid," the tenant of the tower warned him, "to come so close to me? Sit on that stone. I'll go around the other side of this bush, and we can talk without seeing each other. Be careful. Your fingers almost brushed against my hand!"

"I wanted to shake it," said De Maistre.

"It would have been the first time in my life," the leper replied, "that I had had that pleasure. No one has ever taken my hand."

"The unfortunate love to talk about their misfortunes." With these words the leper of the tower resumed his story. His sister had been his only link to the rest of humankind. When that link was broken by the will of the Almighty, he was condemned to eternal solitude. The nature of their illness, however, had forbidden them even that normal intimacy which, in the world outside, unites friends in sorrow. Even when he and his sister prayed together they did not look at each other, for fear that terrible sight would disturb their holy meditations. Their glances met only in heaven. After prayers the companion of his solitude usually returned to her own cell, or disappeared behind the hedge of hazel that bordered the garden.

There was a reason for the austere rule of their life together. When leprosy (to which his whole family had fallen victim) finally struck his sister and brought her to the tower in Aosta, they had never before seen each other. Her eyes widened in awful terror at the sight of her brother. For fear that the sight of him would plunge her into despair and, a hundred times worse, that too-near communion might aggravate her illness, he adopted this pitiful regimen. Leprosy had infected only her breasts, and the last spark of hope was not spent that one day she might recover and leave this habitation of the living dead. There was still some of the trelliswork where, after her arrival, he had erected a partition of hop to divide the garden in two. Narrow paths ran down both sides of the green hedge. The brother and sister could walk along together without seeing one another and without approaching each other too closely.

In spite of everything, he had not been absolutely alone then. In his solitude he heard the sound of her footsteps. When he went out under the trees for his morning prayers, the door of the tower would open silently and her voice would join his. In the afternoon when he tended his flowers, she would sometimes stroll up and down in the setting sun, and her shadow would swing back and forth like a pendulum over the flower beds. And when he did not see her, he found signs of her presence everywhere. One night he was pacing up and down his cell in an attempt to stifle some particularly sharp pains. Tired, he sat down on the bed for a while. In the deathly silence of the night he suddenly heard a slight rustle outside the door. He went to the door, put his ear to it, and understood at once. She was kneeling outside the door and in a barely perceptible whisper was reciting the Miserere. Tears flooded his eyes, he fell to his knees and followed her words with his lips. "Go to bed now," he told her at last. "I feel a little better. God bless you for your compassion." She departed in silence. Indeed, her prayer had been answered, and he had a few hours of peaceful sleep. But now? Now he was all alone again.

After her death he fell into a stupor that deprived him of the power to measure the depth of his loss. When he had recovered sufficiently to understand his new situation, he came near to losing his mind. He remembered this period as doubly painful. For it marked the greatest misfortune he had suffered and it recalled a temptation to crime, conquered only at the last moment.

During other periods of depression the idea of ending his life had occurred to him, but he had always known how to suppress it, at least for a while. And now a poor thing that should not have melted his heart nearly drove him to the verge of suicide.

A little mongrel dog had wandered into the tower a few years before. The leper and his sister had lavished the tenderest care on the poor animal, and after his sister's death the dog was all that was left to him. It must have been the dog's ugliness that led it to the haven of the Tower of Fright. Driven out by the living, it was a veritable treasure in the house of the dead. The leper and his sister called the dog *Miracolo* because its perpetual gaiety sometimes gave them a fleeting moment of forgetfulness. Although the dog would run off for long periods, it never occurred to its new master that these adventures might alarm the citizens of Aosta. One day two soldiers knocked at the gate of the tower with orders to drown the four-legged vagabond at once in the Dora River. They tied a rope around the dog's neck and dragged it to the gate. But the crowd assembled outside begrudged the mongrel that end in the clean billows of the Dora and stoned it to death just outside the gate.

At the sound of the howling crowd, the leper ran to his cell more dead than alive. His legs gave out beneath him, and he threw himself on the bed. All the old wounds of his heart seemed to open afresh.

In that state of mind he waited until sunset before going to his favorite corner of the garden. The friendly landscape was calming him when he suddenly spied a pair of lovers on the path near the wall. They walked along immersed in their happiness, stopping every few feet to embrace in peaceful security, never suspecting that an envious glance was tracking them and almost devouring them. Yes, envious! Never before had a picture of human felicity presented itself so vividly to the tenant of the tower, and for the first time envy crept into his heart. He immediately returned to his cell. Oh God, how desolate and bleak, how terrible it seemed now! "Then it is here," he exclaimed, "that I am doomed to live forever. Dragging my miserable life behind me, it is here that I must await the end of my days! The Almighty floods every living creature with torrents of felicity and only I . . . I am the only creature that must live alone. What an atrocious fate!"

Overwhelmed by these sad thoughts, he forgot the one comforter that still remained to him—himself. "Why," he continued his blasphemous monologue, "did I ever see the light of day? Why should I be nature's only stepchild? Like a disinherited son I look on the rich heritage of all mankind, and heaven in its niggardliness denies only me my share. No, no," his wrath overflowed, "there is no happiness for you on this earth. Die, you miserable wretch, die! You have befouled the earth with your presence too long. Let the earth swallow you alive. Let every trace of your being disappear behind you." His unrestrained fury increased every minute. His only thought was self-destruction.

He decided to burn the tower and entrust the immolation of the last traces of his existence to the flames. In his despair he went outside the gate of the tower and wandered around the foot of the wall. Shouts burst from his breast against his will and terrified him in the silence of the night. On the verge of madness, he withdrew toward the gate and screamed, "Woe to you, Leper, woe to you!" And as if everything conspired to his ruin, suddenly from the direction of the fortress of Bramafan an echo repeated clearly, "Woe to you!" He stopped at the gate and looked behind him. The faint echo of the mountains picked it up for a long while, "Woe to you!"

He took a lamp, gathered some dry wood and twigs for kindling, and went to the lowest room of the tower, the room that had been his sister's when she was alive. He had not been in there since her death. Everything looked as if she had died only the day before. He set the lamp on the table and noticed the crucifix she had always worn around her neck. The ribbon of the crucifix was folded between the leaves of the Bible on the table. He froze at the sight and suddenly realized the profundity of the crime he was about to commit. Mechanically he opened the Bible. A sealed letter fell out. "I will soon leave you alone," she had written, "but I will never forsake you. I will watch over you from heaven. And I will beseech God that He give you courage to bear this life with resignation until it pleases Him to reunite us in a better world. I leave you this cross, which I wore all my life. It brought me consolation in pain and was the only witness to my tears. Remember, when you see it, that my last wish was that you could live and die as a good Christian." A cloud seemed to pass before his eyes after reading these last words, and he fainted.

It was the middle of the night when he regained consciousness, and everything that had happened to him during the day seemed like a dream. He turned a thankful glance toward heaven. The sky was calm and clear, and a single star glistened outside the window. Was there not some sign of hope in this, that one of the rays was intended for the leper's cell? He returned to his own room and spent the rest of the night reading the Book of Job, feeling with a kind of joy that the dark fog of madness that had driven him to the verge of mortal sin was finally dispersed.

"Oh, merciful stranger!" the leper suddenly sighed. "May God bless you and may you never have to live alone!"

He thought for a moment and added: "She was only twenty-five when she died, but her sufferings made her much older. In spite of the illness that distorted her features, she still would have been beautiful had it not been for that terrible pallor . . . She was the living effigy of death. I couldn't look at her without trembling . . . She suffered so terribly that I watched the end approach with a desperate joy . . ."

When he had finished, the leper buried his face in his hands. After a moment of silence, he got up and said to De Maistre, "If you are ever caught in the snares of pain and grief, good sir, remember the lonely man of Aosta. Then your visit will not have been in vain."

They walked to the gate together. Before going out into the street, De Maistre put on his right glove and again offered to shake his host's hand. The leper jumped back in fright. He raised his hands to heaven and cried out: "Merciful God, lavish all good things on this compassionate traveler."

De Maistre asked if they might write to each other every now and then, taking the necessary precautions, of course. For the twinkling of an eye the leper hesitated. "Why," he replied then, "seek refuge in illusions? I can have no other companion than myself and no other friend than God. Goodbye, kind stranger, goodbye. And may God be with you . . . Goodbye for ever!"

The visitor went out. The leper closed the gate and locked it.

III

The nearby Alps temper the heat of summer in these parts, but at the same time they smother the visitor from the lowlands in a kind of dreamlike numbness. The quiet is absolute. Occasionally a bird may fall from somewhere and, rebounding hard from the ground, disappear among the green treetops like a loose stone from the mountain slope that for a moment breaks the dark and motionless surface of a lake. Or the ear may catch the faint tinkle of a bell in a distant pasture, like the echo from the bottom of a well. Only at twilight, when the sun beyond the mountains reddens briefly with a cool luster and disappears, does the first gentle breeze penetrate the dense, sticky air that covers the valley all day with an opaline film.

Anyone looking for solitude will not be disappointed among these hills. The Italians call them *colline*; the word is as fluent and melodious as the shape and golden green color of the melancholy hills themselves. During my leave here, I never saw a human face during the day. In the evening I would go to the village and sit for several hours in the tavern, where the Piedmontese peasants in their big hats drank the local, almost black wine and sang their guttural songs to the crescent moon that shone through the leaves.

In the first days of September it rained. Torrents of water beat against the walls of the house and against the trembling window panes, and hammered an arpeggio across the loose tiles of the roof. The afternoons were dark, and the sky hung low over the Elvo valley like a gray rag wrung out in an enormous washtub by a pair of hands hidden in the clouds. Sometimes the sky cleared for a while in the morning. Even then the rain did not always stop, but turned into a sunny spray of silver drops. Clouds formed a frayed woolen collar halfway up the Mucrone; the peak itself towered above them, fresh and clean in contrast with the ashen steppes below. The dark-green leaves on the trees glittered like bottle glass, and the valley looked like the bottom of a drained pool covered with pondweed.

Sometimes out of boredom and sometimes as if I owed it to the intangible genius of the house, I read again and again the little book by De Maistre I had found on the table. Often, particularly at night, after having read the last words, I would turn away from the dirty walls hung with etchings and broken by the shadows of the furniture, and with relief I would look at the moths gathered on the ceiling over the pale circle of the lampshade. After a while my habitual reading of that book began to call up the same reminiscences. Near the town in Poland where I was born, there is a high mountain dear to the hearts of tourists. It is called the Holy Cross for the relics apparently preserved in the old Bernardine abbey at the peak. At the base of the mountain, by the side of the road leading to the nearest human settlement, there is a stone statue facing toward the abbey. It is the kneeling figure of the "Pilgrim of the Holy Cross," believed by authorities on the region to be an ex-voto set there centuries ago by some pious pilgrim.

Folklore, however, has enveloped the stone pilgrim in legend: every year the kneeling figure advances the space of a poppy seed, and when he finally reaches the summit of the Holy Cross, the world will end. Evidently the contemplation of ultimate things was not foreign to the creators of this legend. Nor—far more surprising—were they strangers to the subtler relationships between hope and hopelessness, faith and despair. Because it is equally legitimate to conclude that—in his endless suffering, cutting his knees on the stones at every step—the Pilgrim of the Holy Cross will one day reach and yet never reach the end of his journey. If he reaches the summit, the only reward for his perseverance will be a momentary vision of the light of salvation before the last fire consumes him along with the whole world.

The stone pilgrim has no face, just a small rough head set directly on the torso. The forehead and nose form a continuous vertical line with the beard. There are two holes for eyes: like those of a blind man, they stare ahead without seeing. His hair hangs down over his arms, which are set unnaturally low on the torso, and his hands are crossed in a pious gesture on his breast. The broad base of the kneeling figure is overgrown with moss. Corroded by wind and rain, chunks of stone chipped away, he is a monument of infinite patience. But only when one sees people who pass by every day, indifferent to the stone figure as if it were a piece of the landscape long unnoticed, does one realize that the pilgrim must also be infinitely lonely.

It was precisely this, aside from his physical appearance, that led my imagination to connect him with the leper of the tower in Aosta.

IV

In the beginning I thought that the former occupant of the house in which I was staying had been attracted by the peculiar solace contained in De Maistre's little book.

The preface to the Neapolitan edition of 1828 suggested that view. The translator had written it in the then-fashionable form of a dedication. The Princess of Torella, Duchess of Lavello, etc., to whom the translation was dedicated, was implored by her humble servant to accept the Italian version of the book that had given so much pleasure to Count Flemming, the Prussian ambassador to the Kingdom of Naples, when he was alive. "It is fitting that the ambassador's untimely death," the translator wrote, "painful to everyone, but most painful to you, Madame, be commemorated in this manner." For Count Flemming had often said that there was no man on earth, no matter how terrible his misery, who would not consider himself fortunate in comparison with that leper. The count called this book the comforter of the afflicted, and since the count himself was victim to pain and affliction he kept that book with him as if it were a vial of ever-soothing balm. The Princess of Torella shared the ambassador's enthusiasm for the book, and it was from her that the translator had come to know of the existence of De Maistre's account.

What touched the translator most deeply when he read the book was the gesture of renunciation with which the tenant of the tower in Aosta declined to shake hands or establish a correspondence with De

Maistre. With courage and resignation the leper had accepted his dual cross of patience and solitude—a challenge to our whining epoch, and a magnificent example to those who consider that the nobler answer to misfortune is not complaint and lamentation, but silence—the silence that is nourished by the strength of the soul and looks only to God for its reward.

Could there have been any doubt that the lonesome recluse in his little tower on the steppes of the Mucrone nourished himself day after day on a few drops of this ever-soothing balm?

To be sure, I soon discovered that I was mistaken. I found a notebook in the drawer of the table that indicated the *ginnasio* teacher's concern with the matter went far deeper. To this day I cannot say what end that notebook was intended for—literary, historical, or philosophical—because it included only summaries and extracts of various kinds and not a word concerning the writer.

What I supposed to be the title of the intended work was printed in Latin on the first page: VITA DUM SUPEREST, BENE EST. The succeeding pages—sometimes bearing only a single line at the top, sometimes covered half-way down by his almost illegible script —gave no clue to whether the title was written in bitter mockery, or whether it represented the old man's confession of faith. Actually, the former occupant's notes gave no clear notion of anything at all. Their very randomness rather suggested the chaotic nature of his reflections and study. In one place he had copied down the real name and date of death of the leper of Aosta: Pier Bernardo Guasco, who died in 1803, six years after De Maistre's visit. In another place he had transcribed Octave Mirbeau's observation that leprosy is a disease from which a man neither recovers nor dies. Just under this observation, which belongs to the tradition of leprosy as a "mystical disease," was a quotation from Kierkegaard:

It is indeed very far from being true that, literally understood, one dies of this sickness, or that this sickness ends with bodily death. On the contrary, the torment of despair is precisely this, not to be able to die. So it has much in common with the situation of the moribund when he lies and struggles with death, and cannot die. So to be sick unto death is, not to be able to die—yet not as though there were hope of life; no, the hopelessness in this case is that even the last hope, death, is not available. When death is the greatest danger, one hopes for life; but when one becomes acquainted with an even more dreadful danger, one hopes for death. So when the danger is so great that death has become one's hope, despair is the disconsolateness of not being able to die.

Further on, there were a few verses from the Book of Leviticus, 13: 45–46:

And the leper in whom the plague is, his clothes shall be rent, and his head bare, and he shall put a covering upon his upper lip, and shall cry, Unclean, unclean. All the days wherein the plague shall be in him he shall be defiled; he is unclean: he shall dwell alone; without the camp shall his habitation be.

I was most interested by two long extracts from the seventeenth-century documents, describing the condition of lepers in the Middle Ages, that Ambroise Paré found in the Hôtel Dieu archives in Paris. One was the medieval *Decalog of the Leper*, which forbade the leper, by order of the king, everything that might even indirectly bring him in contact with his fellow men, in other words, everything except living and breathing. One of the provisions, however, allowed the leper to answer questions if he turned his face in the direction of the wind. The other document was a description of the leper's "investiture," or rather his temporal interment. Wearing the stole and surplice, the priest would await him on the threshold of the church. Then the priest would read to him publicly the medical certificate that declared him, on the basis of the prescribed symptoms, a leper before the law. Later the same priest would sprinkle the leper with holy water and clear a path for him through the crowd into the House of God. The church would be hung with shrouds, and a catafalque would be erected by the main altar for the occasion. After the funeral mass for the peace of his soul, the leper would be wrapped in a white sheet, laid on a litter, and accompanied by the whole congregation to the cemetery. By a freshly dug grave the priest would sprinkle a handful of dirt on the leper's head and recite the sacramental formula: "With this sign you are dead to the world. You will be born again in God. Therefore have patience, the patience of Christ and His Saints, until the day you enter into Paradise, where there is no affliction, where all are pure and beautiful, without blemish or stain, more brilliant in splendor than the sun." At the end the priest would carefully hand the leper a hooded cloak, a basket, a pail, and a stick with three sliding discs, pronouncing the following sacramental formula: "Take this attire and wear it in humility. The basket and pail for food and water. And the rattle that you may warn passersby in time of your presence."

There was one word in the private notes of the house below the Mucrone that might have unveiled something of the sentiments or thoughts of the lonely teacher, but unfortunately that word was too ambiguous. The faithful reader of De Maistre's account had circled the passage on the last page that described the leper's hesitation (for the twinkling of an eye) before declining the offer to exchange letters. And in the margin he had written *Perchè?*, "Why?" It only caught my attention after I had read the notebook I found on the table. Did the word express surprise that the leper of Aosta did not jump at the offer, and did it allude to the Latin phrase on the title page of the notebook? Or did it express disapproval that the leper had hesitated at all, albeit for an instant, instead of bearing bravely and with resignation his "dual cross of patience and solitude," without betraying a shade of fear at the prospect of that eternal silence which "is nourished by the strength of the soul and looks only to God for its reward?" To this day, in spite of everything I learned in the nearby village about my dead host, I cannot answer these questions. But neither can I answer other questions, questions concerning De Maistre's interlocutor himself. Did the pulse of hope, however faint, beat again in that brief flash of hesitation? Did Pier Bernardo Guasco come to life for the last time, if only for an instant, in the creature who as the *Lebbroso* had died to the world years before?

The rains stopped as unexpectedly as they had begun. The end of summer in the sub-Alpine region of Italy is barely distinguishable from the hot and protracted beginning of autumn, which often lasts to the end of October and subsides slowly in the lazy ripeness of the mountain sun. Only in November do the chilly mornings announce a cooler season.

The rustling ribbons of the falling streams, silver in the bright sun, seemed to wash away the dark reflections of my reading. But they only seemed to do so, because a few days after the weather cleared I gave in to the temptation to make a trip, the only point of which could be to touch a tombstone that was sinking into the earth.

V

The town of Ivrea is nominally the entry into the Val d'Aosta but the true valley only begins farther on, at the Chateau d'Issogne, a fifteenth-century example of Late Gothic architecture built by the Counts of Challant—the same family that, according to popular legend, produced the assassin of the Duchess of Braganza in the tower of Bramafan.

The entrance to the Val d'Aosta must seem to every traveler to be the jumping-off place from a realm of light into a domain of darkness, guarded on both sides by the heavy shadow of the cliffs. There are valleys where the light of day only creeps in through mountain passes, but in the Val d'Aosta it emerges as if from underground. One cannot guess the age of a passerby wading through the darkness only a few feet away. Italians call the Aosta valley *la valle tetra*. And it is gloomy, indeed, although such a commonplace word does scant justice to the sullen beauty of that narrow streak of shadow dividing two worlds. As one goes on, his eyes gradually become accustomed to the dark, and he fixes his gaze on the dim strip of fog suspended above the waters of the mountain stream, which smash against the unyielding rock wall with a thunderous roar.

At Saint-Vincent the valley brightens and assumes a more cheerful tone. But along the road that winds monotonously through the chestnut woods and deserted pastures on the slopes, and on to the bridge over the Dora, *la valle tetra* again justifies its name. Beyond the river the deep basin of the actual valley of Aosta springs open. Saturated with the green of vineyards and flatlands, splotched here and there by small settlements and isolated houses, the valley resembles a painter's palette. And for a moment the traveler forgets that nature has imprisoned this colored bowl in a dead fist of naked peaks and glaciers. But the town with its severe air will remind him.

Aosta—the ancient Augusta Praetoria—owes its severity not only to the Roman and medieval ruins that stand like old stumps in the new city. The streets are narrow, but they lack the theatrical bustle of the back streets of southern Italian cities, and the houses have a stiff and repelling cleanliness about them. The people have hard, cloudy faces, and even in moments of animation maintain a heavy dignity that one associates with Protestant rather than Catholic countries. One senses some particular harmony between this human climate and the rocky and ascetic peace of the collegiate church of St. Orso. The city of Aosta is closed on all sides. Beyond the tollgates of most of the roads leading out of the city is a massive and formidable wall of Alps. The road leading to the Great St. Bernard Pass, for example, is simply a prolongation of Xavier de Maistre Street.

Time does all, it erases even the memory of human sufferings. In spite of De Maistre Street, in spite of the Via Torre del Lebbroso, in spite of the fact that Aosta is still essentially a small town, no one I asked could point out exactly the road to the tower where the leper Pier Bernardo Guasco spent twenty-one years of his life. A century and a half had passed since his ceaseless silent agony had received its ultimate reward from God—a century and a half of life, death, birth, and again life and death. A century and a half had passed since the solitary inhabitant of that unreal world isolated beyond the borders of existence had disappeared—a century and a half in which the real world bestirred itself, day after day, month after month, year after year, about its griefs and joys. Is it any wonder, then, that the crest of time's eternal tide had obliterated the memory of the tower, or that the deafening roar of that sea had smothered its silent voice?

It turned out that the other tower, Bramafan, was better known in Aosta. But night had fallen, and the street leading from the railway station to Bramafan was poorly lighted and deserted. In this still sparsely settled quarter of the city (as it had been in De Maistre's day), looking like the outskirts of any provincial town—crooked fences, neglected gardens, houses scarcely rising above the ground, and black coal smoke near the tower—the Cry of Hunger had never abated in the course of centuries. The round tower rose dramatically from the darkness against a background of low floating clouds, which every now and then uncovered a glimpse of the moon, like the flashing glow of a distant blaze.

The pavement suddenly ended and a footpath led off at an angle between the houses that bordered the open fields. Fifty yards farther on, the path entered a small empty square, and disappeared in a narrow alley on the other side. It was even darker here, but at the far end of the alley I could see the pale glow of the lights of the center of town. I stopped half way down the alley at the sight of a wall more than six feet high.

I had no difficulty in recognizing the sharp rectangularity of the tower and the mute eminence—so well rendered by the anonymous author of the etching—of the stone crown on top. Standing on tiptoe I could see, through the only breach in the wall, part of a yard grown wild with weeds that had once been the leper's garden.

Even in old and long-abandoned cemeteries one does not see such an accumulation of dead mold. The foot of the building was smothered with thick, overgrown stalks and enormous leaves. The walls exhaled the dust that powders tombstones sinking slowly into the ground. The highest window, just under the crest of the tower, was boarded up; the others were black, like hollowed-out eye sockets. But the silence of the place was not altogether dead, and it was this that was disturbing. There was something of the suspended, unfinished, unreconciled about it. It was hard not to fancy that there was someone walled up in there, someone with his ear pressed against a fissure in the stones, listening for sounds of life. The handle of the gate was rusted in its fixture; it had been a long time since anyone had turned it.

The Allied uniform opened all doors in Italy after the war: the next morning the municipal usher from the Ufficio delle Antichità e Belle Arti accompanied me to the tower. The day was sunny and almost hot. If one knows the way, it is only five minutes from Chanoux Square in the center of town to the corner of the alley marked Via Torre del Lebbroso.

It must always have been the street of shoemakers and small craftsmen, for all along the way low, arched entries curved over the artisans' bent backs. Our steps could not be heard over the din of hammers and the whistle of planes, and not a single head peeked out at us from the shops. But several children attached themselves to us, kicking a ball back and forth behind us. Years before, another group of children had fallen on the flower beds in the garden beyond the wall, and had run off at once shouting, *Buon giorno, Lebbroso!* What was it in those laughing shouts that had given the leper such peculiar satisfaction?

The tower lost much of its strangeness by day, but it still mournfully suggested a corner of a cemetery overgrown with weeds and nettles. Stones have an inexplicable quality of their own: they age in one way when they patiently serve man, and in another way when they are ignored by the stream of life.

Abandoned by man the stones seem to dry and crack like a crust of earth untouched for years by a drop of water. Visited by man they thicken and harden like the bark of an eternally green tree—even when man's presence is only his memory and not his solicitous hand.

I approached the tower with the same emotion I had felt on my visit the night before. But now the tower seemed to imprison not so much the forgotten hermit as his whole, vast, inhuman desert without horizons. The only human sign there, the only thing that somehow bound this shred of earth to the world around and acknowledged an interrupted life—rather than a mere void that had existed since time immemorial—was something about the broken, moldering steps that had been cut out of the remains of Roman wall to the left of the hedge.

Inside the tower I could not immediately distinguish the staircase from the rubbish heaped against the wall. It was like being at the bottom of a deep rocky pit, and it took a long while before I could formulate an idea of the place from the play of patches of light, the shadows, and the black recesses. The air was hung with the musty and pungent odor of dampness and decomposition.

Fortunately the stairs turned out to be more stable

than I had supposed. Without touching the railing, and bracing my back against the damp wall, I climbed slowly until at last I was able to grasp the ledge of a small window. From there I saw a part of the courtyard and my guide, who had unbuttoned his jacket and was stretched out on the grass with his face to the sun. The stairs cut through the floor above and gave onto a landing illuminated by a sliver of light that came through a half-open door. I opened the door but did not enter: it was the lowest room of the tower, the room in which the leper's sister had lived.

A ray of light fell directly on another flight of stairs at the opposite end of the vestibule. The first steps creaked so menacingly that I wanted to turn back. And again the darkness thickened. But as I stood undecided, I heard a rapid beating of wings just over my head, and a narrow opening appeared above me as if cut by a knife. A fissure of light came through the door a bird had thrust open in its flight. There remained one sign of its presence in the room on the highest landing of the tower—a loose board in the window was still swinging on its upper nails from the violent blow. I pushed the board to one side and saw the gentle landscape of meadows beyond the railroad, strewn here and there with the remains of the morning fog and ribbons of smoke from burned leaves.

The small cell was rectangular, and only now I saw that there was a second window, covered with a piece of cloth. It opened onto the town and the garland of hills under the Great St. Bernard Pass, and the white peaks beyond. The campanile of the collegiate church and the octagonal turret of the cloister of St. Orso seemed to leap forward from the Alpine background of light, clear crystal. What the former inhabitant of the tower probably never knew was that the pride of that church was a centuries-old painting hanging on the left wall of the apse, *La miracolosa guarigione di una storpia nella chiesa e processione,* "The Miraculous Healing of a Lame Woman in the Church, and Procession"; and that three phases of the plagues of Job were carved on the capital of one of the columns of the Romanesque portico in the cloister.

A low, bare cot, almost fallen to the ground, stood in the corner between the windows. Against the wall on the other side of the cell, behind a massive table and a leather-covered stool, stood a long carved chest, the kind the Piedmont peasants use as a cupboard, as a bench, and, if necessary, as a cot for the night. The ceiling turned down obliquely over an earthenware stove. The whole cell suggested a narrow cage—movement within the cell was limited to an absolute minimum.

The central point of the cell, however, was a large crucifix. It did not hang above the head of the bed but at the side, so that one could kneel on the floor to pray and prop one's elbows on the bed. A magnificent wrought-iron figure of Christ, though out of all proportion, hung on a wide-armed cross painted ebony. At first glance, the coarseness of the iron, the distorted swelling of the ribs, and the blotches of rust and encrusted dirt, all seemed to be ulcers covering the entire body of Christ. Instead of a crown of thorns, what seemed like a large black wedding ring was pressed on the exaggeratedly bent head of the Christ.

VI

The Italian assigned to our military mission in Milan did not tell the whole truth about his distant relative in the little house under the Mucrone; but perhaps no one knows the whole truth. Nevertheless, it was decidedly too little to say only that the old pensioner had died there all alone toward the end of the war. After having heard the accounts given in the nearby village, after my return from Aosta, I began to take the word "died" with a grain of salt; the word was correct insofar as the physical fact was concerned. Only the qualification, "all alone," was absolutely right—dreadfully right.

Not much was known of the *ginnasio* teacher's past. He was Sicilian by birth, and before he was sent to Turin he had taught in Sicily, where he lost his entire family—his wife and three children—in the famous Messina earthquake of 1908. It was rumored that he had been retired prematurely because of the scandal arising from an attempt at suicide. He had bought this house in 1938 from the village doctor (a widower who went to live with his sons in Turin) and had moved in at once.

In the last six years of his life he was seen in the village only a few times in all. He spoke to no one except his regular provisioners, and he never acknowledged the greetings that are directed even to strangers in these parts. Although he was entirely gray he was still vigorous, and his not overly tall, lean figure commanded a certain irresistible respect. Perhaps there had been a trace of fear in this respect, for his eyes sometimes glittered with a hidden madness. Sicilians are known for their natural inclination to the tragic. It is said that Sicilians "carry the thought of death with them always, like a thorn in the flesh." The old man's house came to be known as *La bara siciliana*, the Sicilian coffin. Later the name was shortened to

La bara, and this name stuck. Once a month the local postman brought a pension check from the post office to *La bara*. Every Saturday morning the innkeeper's daughter took the bus to *La bara* with a basket of provisions and laundry; *il padrone della bara* waited for her even in the worst weather at the crossing of the road and the path up the slope to the house, and helped her carry up the basket.

Once the young priest from the village visited him. The interview in the garden was brief, and the priest remained standing. He asked the old man why he never went to mass on Sundays. Without lifting his head from the clipped hedges, the old man replied that he did not feel the need to go; what he was waiting for did not require faith—only patience. Asked how he could live that way, he replied with a shrug: "Because I cannot die."

In August 1944 the remains of a shattered S.S. division poured through the countryside seizing men wherever they could to be sent to labor camps in Germany. There already existed something on the order of a partisan information network in the region, and the village on the Mucrone highlands was warned in time. On a Wednesday night all of the men, even the aged, were evacuated to the hills; only the women and children remained behind, and the young priest. Friday morning a large truck escorted by four motorcycles appeared in the little square in front of the church. As soon as the S.S. sergeant saw the women and children being herded into the square, he understood the situation. He decided to teach the women and children, at least, a lesson they would not forget; and he did not lack imagination. Through his driver who knew some Italian, he announced that if they did not produce at least one male inhabitant within two hours, the priest would pay with his life for the men's flight.

No one knows exactly how the lonely house three kilometers from the village came to play a part in this drama of the war: whether one of the women whispered something to the German driver, or whether one of the soldiers had noticed the house from the end of the road. In any case, a motorcycle with a sidecar leapt for the prey and brought it back to the square fifteen minutes later.

Il padrone della bara seemed mystified by what was going on around him. A soldier shoved him forward toward the sergeant, who was sitting on the running board of the truck. The crowd thronged the steps of the church. The old man was calm and, as usual, silent, but at the same time he seemed pale and bewildered. The soldier left him alone in the middle of the square and took several paces off to one side. At the sergeant's command, the soldier lightly raised the barrel protruding from under his right armpit. The crowd of women and children began to sway back and forth with a mournful lament, and the priest began to recite the prayer for the dead. Only then did the old man waver. He threw his arms across his heart, and his trembling face turned whiter than his hair. The plaintive singing stopped, and the sergeant and the soldier aiming his rifle turned to each other without a word. "No, no, no," the old man wailed in a cracking voice. The priest broke off the prayer, looked at him for a moment, and turned to the driver: "He is not to blame. He's not from here. He's not from our village." The old man repeated in a monotone: "I am not to blame. I'm not from here. I'm not from this village." The sergeant asked the interpreter something. "He's from Turin," the priest anticipated his answer. "I'm from Turin," the old man repeated like an echo. No one had ever heard so many words cross his lips.

The rest happened in a flash. The truck and its escort of four motorcycles disappeared around the bend of the road leading toward the city. In the middle of the square—dazzlingly white from the sun and the pastel façades of the church and the little town hall—lay an enormous black bird in a pool of blood, the wings of its cassock spread out like a cross. The crowd of women and children huddled around the church door stood motionless. The old man was standing alone on the other side of the square. He stared at the body of the priest for a long time. Finally he covered his face with his hands and turned toward home.

The crowd of women and children followed him at a distance the whole three kilometers in the scorching August heat and the dust of the winding road that led up to his house. The old man halted often, a few times he stumbled, and once he even fell: he crawled over to the little stone wall and pulled himself up again. The crowd stopped then and waited in silence. The whole affair lasted perhaps an hour. The sun was directly overhead when with an effort the old man pushed open the gate and disappeared behind the trees along the iron fence.

The next day was Saturday, and the innkeeper's daughter did not take him the basket of provisions. But there was no reason to do so. The bus driver did not see him that morning at his usual station at the crossing of the road and the path. Curious, he stopped the bus and walked up to *La bara*. *Il padrone della bara* lay dead on the sofa in his room. His body was already cold.

VII

Several times I have tried to write a story about the last six years of the life of the resident of the tower in Aosta, but I have helplessly laid down my pen halfway through each attempt. Like De Maistre, I could not conceive of eternal solitude. And the idea frightened me, as it had De Maistre.

"Often when we dream," a poet writes, "what we see and experience strikes us as something unreal and at the same time as something more than real. Paralyzed, we hover uncertainly on the border between night and day; when we finally open our eyes, for a fraction of a second we are unsure which of two impressions is the true one: the one that actually disappeared or the one that took its place. I try to think of this immeasurably brief moment of suspense whenever I want to imagine the hour of my death."

Perhaps this is a key to the idea of eternal solitude—that moment of suspension between night and day, between dreaming and waking, drawn out endlessly. Or it is a dream of death, in a tower surrounded by the sea, from which one is awakened by an unfathomable spasm of fright only at the approach of actual death? De Maistre took the motto of his story from *The Seasons*: "Winter," by the eighteenth-century English poet James Thomson. I wanted to use a pair of lines from the "City of Dreadful Night," by his nineteenth-century namesake:

> For life is but a dream whose shapes return
> Some frequently, some seldom, some by night . . .

I never managed to establish the circumstances in which Pier Bernardo Guasco died, although I passed through Aosta many times again after the war. But I happened on two traditions concerning him. One had it that shortly before his death the leper stopped accepting provisions, and by starving himself hastened the end of his days. According to the other, one cloudy March night he went out into the deserted street carrying a lamp in his hand, and some late passerby chased him back to his tower with stones and curses, and he died soon after. I was both touched and amused to detect that unequalled ability of simple people constantly to rework old legends: thus two ancient legends of Aosta were kept alive—the starved Duchess of Braganza in Bramafan, and the white lady of the *Torre dello Spavento*.

I do not regret being unable to write a story about the tenant of the tower. If there were not things in human life that man's imagination refused to comprehend, he would end by cursing the despair that penetrates literature, instead of seeking hope in its productions. But I often think of the leper of Aosta when I close my eyes. I like to imagine him finally dragging himself on his knees to the top of the Holy Cross Mountain, infinitely exhausted and worn out by time, and collapsing with a shout of triumph on the naked rock. The shout will die at once in the deafening roar of the end of the world.

THE
SECOND COMING

A MEDIEVAL TALE

Turning and turning in the widening
  gyre
The falcon cannot hear the falconer;
Things fall apart; the centre cannot
  hold;
Mere anarchy is loosed upon the world.
The blood-dimmed tide is loosed, and
  everywhere
The ceremony of innocence is drowned;
The best lack all conviction, while the
  worst
Are full of passionate intensity.

Surely some revelation is at hand;
Surely the Second Coming is at hand. . . .

W. B. Yeats, "The Second Coming"

I

Plagues and the frailty of human life! As
people stretched their limbs in the morning, they did
not know if the gravedigger would be coming for
them by evening, stopping for the fires burning at
the thresholds of those houses Death had blindly
selected, marking that shred of land through which
he passed. Smoke clouds crept slowly over cities and
countryside; and everywhere the menace touched,
mournful songs and supplicatory invocations of processions, the sprinkling of heads with ashes from the
burned-out track of the Invasion, public choral con-

fessions, and the laying of naked infants at the foot of the altar were daily events. One could see the shadow of the Prince of Darkness lurking in the innocent eyes of maidens. Cruelty fed by fear and exasperation then knew no bounds. Unaccustomed to measuring life by death, the only means at our disposal, simple minds panicked at the sight of so maddening a triumph of chance. A hidden longing for immortality went hand in hand with a conviction that God had brought the faithful flock to the brink of the precipice in order that His wrathful finger might brand the sloth and sluggishness of His shepherds. And everywhere they sought deliverance through asceticism.

On May 4, 1260, a procession of penitents with black sacks over their heads appeared on the streets of Perugia. They were called *disciplinati*, and the holy hermit Fra Raniero Fasani inspired them with the need for repentance. A foreboding of pregnant days hung in the air: it was the year that, according to the prophecy of the Calabrian abbot Giovacchino, was to open the third and last era of the Holy Spirit.

To mark their detachment from the world they donned dark hoods and went slowly, their bare feet groping step by step over the scorned earth. They sang *laudi*, invoking God's charity with sounds that resembled the howling of animals. They cursed the works of life and earthly love and lashed each other with switches. They proclaimed the heavenly hail of punishment and vengeance and gropingly stretched their fearfully trembling hands toward the crucifixes and pictures borne at the head of the procession. They stabbed and tore their own bodies with hooks. They beat themselves in circling groups animated by a dance of frenzy and horror. They roused the memory of the Lord's Passion as they looked steadfastly to the longed-for Kingdom of the Spirit. Once outside the city gates, their example tore men from the plough, leaving the land deserted behind them as their ranks grew. From the heights of Perugia one could see them on the horizon in the evening, lighting their torches by small fires; seeking the eternal light, they walked in darkness. At the first great crossroads, like a cut-up snake, they crawled off in the four directions of the earth, which was drying up and cracking without the dew of salvation. Within a few months they appeared in the streets of Rome, Arezzo, and Bologna, on the highroads of the Veneto, Emilia, Liguria, and Piedmont, everywhere recruiting new men to replace the dead abandoned on their march. In the course of a few years the echo of their steps had cut through the barrier of the Alps, calling followers to them in German, Czech, and Polish lands. Everywhere their step resounded, it was a step chasing the perverse Enemy from this earth. Everywhere their voice rang, it was a voice of warning against Satan.

Meanwhile, to be sure, the Prince of Darkness was not asleep. Despair, helplessness, and fear unbolted the heart to asceticism, but also to asceticism's inseparable companion: the seducer of the abyss. The uncertainty of the day and hour incited to transgression and crime. Bodies that were spared by the pyres and cremation burned themselves up in fever, consumed by the flame of sin. Hands grabbed for the jug brimful of the promise of forgetfulness and numbness. Women possessed by the devil ran screaming out of their houses, tearing off their clothes. In the dead of night, knives were sharpened for murder, poison was readied, and treason was plotted. Life was a disordered struggle in traps. Never yet had man exhibited so glaringly his innate wretchedness, entangled with the eternal, yet eternally unsatisfied, yearning for holiness.

II

Although the scourge of God had not yet fallen on Orvieto, Pope Urban IV knew that here too the breath of the storm was approaching: it meant nothing that for the moment there were no lightning flashes or thunder. From the window of the Palazzo Vescovile, where he was residing, he often chanced to look out between the curtains on the crowd in the square. It was a restless and excited crowd, like wild grass blown now to one side now to another at the approach of heavy rain clouds. Eyes looked furtively toward the balcony of the Palazzo, as if seeking some sign. And there were furtive whispers. When in his *sedia gestatoria* sowing on both sides the blessing of the cross, Urban floated over the crowd of heads to one of the churches—to Santa Maria Prisca, to San Lorenzo de Arari, to San Domenico, to San Francesco, or to San Giovenale—he could not suppress the sensation that the curved backs bent too violently and too impatiently, like sea waves tossed by the first shudder of the darkening sky.

He avoided Sant'Andrea, keeping from himself and from the others the memory of that predecessor who a half century earlier had proclaimed the Fourth Crusade from the pulpit of that church. What did Urban himself have to offer to lips thirsting for the living water of miracles, to glances in which the fear of specters lurking somewhere near shone with the cruel star of unnourished faith? He tried to recall the terrible diatribe that the initiator of the Fourth Crusade had written in the *De Miseria Humanae Conditionis* when he was still Lotharius Diaconus. "What will I say of the unfortunate who for countless generations have been tortured to death? They are beaten with rods, they are chopped to pieces with swords, they are burned in flames, they are stoned, they are torn by falcons, they are hanged from gibbets, they are torn apart by tigers, they are scourged with scorpions, they are strung up by ropes, they are imprisoned in dungeons, they are mortified by starvation, they are thrown down from heights, they are drowned, their skin is torn off them, they are dragged on the ground, they are sawed up, they are trampled on. Death to whom? Death to this man! To whom the knife? The knife to this man! Hunger to whom? Starvation to this man! Prison to whom? Prison to this man! To a cruel judgment, to a cruel punishment, to a sad spectacle: to annihilation for the birds of the sky, the beasts of the earth, and the fish of the sea. Woe unto you, woe, woe, mournful mothers who brought into the world such unfortunate sons!"

At night Urban suffered from insomnia. Although he was only sixty-three, he considered it a sign of his imminent summons to the throne of the Almighty. Praying vainly for the blessing of sleep, he got some relief for his cough by resting in a half-sitting position on four pillows. By the light of the single candle burning in the niche by the bed, he would stare at the brocade of the baldaquin above him. Or he would gaze at the dark, attenuated by the small crystal panels of the Gothic window before him. The town slept, its silence broken only by the steps of the night sentries. From below, from the encampments laid out in a tight ring around the hill of Orvieto, sometimes rose the barking of dogs or the broken shouts of men. These sounds of life brought him a strange, bitter solace.

There was wisdom in understanding that there is no great difference between the faith that overflows the river banks and its dried-up bed. From Urban's reign, however, the people expected proof that he was worthy of being the anointed of Him who gave His body for the life of the world. Death was the real fisher of men, but death also excited in them that hunger which changes hope into despair, love into hate, reflection into madness, humility into violence. Where hostile elements lived so near each other, one would have needed to multiply the miraculous loaf many times to satisfy the hungry.

Sleeplessness would numb Urban's whole body. In his random rounds of thought, in his aimless strolls through scenes of memory or imagination, he usually ended at a point at which, like an exhausted wanderer, he would sink into a suddenly opened abyss beneath his feet rather than fall asleep. He would wake up after two or three hours, knowing that no prayers could put him back to sleep. All he could do was wait until the small bulging panes sparkled with the first rays of dawn.

To shorten the last hours of his enforced vigil, he would go down to the garden behind the Palazzo Vescovile. Day would begin to appear almost negligently, the still invisible fingers of the sun unwinding the swaddling clouds of night, but just as the moment of dawn approached, the light would suddenly burst forth with a force that it only matched again just before it was extinguished at the gates of twilight. Was the Creator reminding man, with Nature as His witness, that nowhere does light win such shining victory as it does at the frontiers of night and day?

As far as the eye could see, white orchids of smoke blossomed above the tents of the encampment. Traffic awoke on the roads. At dawn yellow-green Umbria embraced Orvieto with glittering golden arms.

III

One of the last dawns of July in the year 1263, Urban looked out on the road from Bolsena and saw a black blotch that grew rapidly as it neared Orvieto. It was accompanied by a continually growing cry, like the barking of dogs or a call to arms. The closer it came the more clearly one could see the crowd of people thronging around something or someone in the middle. The front of the procession came up backwards, as if the people could not even for a moment tear their eyes from their quarry. More people continued to join the crowd from all sides. Some were pushed off the road and crawled back up its slope on all fours.

When the throng was on an almost perpendicular line below the garden of the Palazzo Vescovile, the Pope finally saw the young man in a habit torn to shreds. Insulted, spit upon, shoved by tens of hands, driven forward by blows, the young man stumbled forward, barefoot and head bowed. He was pulled, or rather dragged, by a rope that had been tied around his wrists.

The young man had been a priest in Bolsena for a short time. He was tormented, as he imprudently admitted, by doubts whether Christ is physically present in the Eucharist. For this, his sentence was to be publicly pilloried for seven days without food. And if the punishment inflicted did not bring back to God this soul corrupted by heresy, he was to be banished for life. They suspended him in an iron cage at the top of the tallest tower in Orvieto, the *Torre del Papa* (the Pope's Tower).

IV

The tower was 150 feet tall. A square structure with a few small window openings to light the spiral staircase, the tower looked like a naked execution stake. Halfway up, it had prison cells for those who were no longer to see the light of God's day. A covered gallery went round the tower. Here the cubical cage of the pillory was exhibited on a long, thick, iron-gray angling rod.

The tower dominated Orvieto and drew the townsmen's glances from every side. By day it stood out like a stake driven into the living body of the city. At night it seemed a skeleton of stone and, like a half-abandoned beehive, it rustled in the silence with the moan of its prisoners.

Passersby gathered in the round courtyard at the foot of the tower whenever the pillory was in use. What was intended as an object of public derision often reminded the gaping crowd of the sculptured angels that architects would set under church arches. The tower was so tall and the courtyard so narrow that when one looked up, an immensity of sky was the only background to the figure of the prisoner with his outstretched hands clasping the bars. But even that vision did not allay the crowd's increasing exasperation. On the contrary—the remains of human compassion were crushed by the fact that a condemned man dared to remind one of the heavenly messengers, that involuntarily he played the role of a mocking angel joker. The fists waved at him cut the air as if armed with spears.

The sun was the only torturer of the heretic of Bolsena, the people could no longer reach him. At first he sat on the wood floor of his cage with his head bowed on his knees and shielded by his folded arms. He spent two whole days in this position, insensible to the flogging of the hot Umbrian July. Had he not been so clearly cramped and strained, he might have been taken for dead. He did not move even when the guard came up to the gallery and poked him with a rod to offer him a sponge to moisten his lips. The disappointed crowd would thin away and then thicken again, impatiently awaiting the highest delight of human cruetly—the fully unveiled picture of another's suffering and degradation. Looking up, all they could see was an immense spider suspended on a thread, a spider who could not or would not swallow up its offering.

Finally, toward evening of the second day, the condemned man stirred from his immobility. Without rising or looking down, he bent forward on his knees. He prayed, with his profile continuing the line of his folded hands. The reddening sunset outlined him with the sharpness of a burin. Then, to the sound of insults and shouts, which now increased in force, darkness mercifully covered him with its black cloak. Several torches that had been brought were no longer able to rend the veil. The night was moonless.

The next morning the reassembled crowd relished the first fruits of its vigil. It was almost noon when the cage trembled from the jerk, and they saw its prisoner convulsively catch hold of the rod with the sponge on its end. He sank his mouth deep into the damp sponge, breathing rapidly as if shaken by spasms. Then he let go of the sponge and sat down again in the same position as before. But his audience did not fail to notice that he continued to breathe convulsively, as if he were sobbing.

In the early afternoon of the next-to-last day of the week, when only a couple of beggars dozed beneath the Pope's Tower, a cry cut the silent hour. The startled beggars tore themselves away from the wall, frightened off. Still half drunk with sleep and with the heat, at first they thought they had imagined the violent swinging of the cage and the unconscious struggling of its prisoner. It was as if their dreams had brought forth the scene they had waited for as they begged under the walls of the tower—a sight that would prove there was someone in the world who must envy even their lot.

At last the apostate of Bolsena felt the sun's invisible noose.

The sound that ripped from his throat was less a scream than the laugh of a madman. He raged wildly, as if his five-day battle against the torture devised for him by his fellow men had taken away his reason. He leapt all over the cage and caught at the bars, gesturing like a monkey. He jumped to the middle of the cage, shielded his naked head with his hands, and hurled blasphemies at the indifferent skies. The next moment he sank to the floor and, heedless of the copiously flowing blood, passionately beat his forehead on the boards. With his face smeared with blood, his mad dance, and his cry of despair laced with laughter, what was he now but the very effigy of the devil, finally forced to cast off his mask. Nothing remained of the irritating illusion of angelic appearance that the pillory atop the Pope's Tower bestowed on its victims.

All that was missing were tongues of fire issuing from the mouth of the possessed man and lightning sparks flashing under his feet.

But the crowd summoned by the shouts to the last act of the spectacle, instead of loudly savoring the longed-for moment drop by drop, stood in silent indecision. All the hidden fear of an age was suddenly reflected, as if by a distorting mirror, in the figure of the devilish buffoon threatening heaven and men. It did not last long. When the prisoner of the cage fell as if thunderstruck and no longer rose, the crowd shook off its fleeting haze of pity. They demanded his corpse; they wanted to tear it to pieces and throw it to the dogs for annihilation.

V

The people erected a pyre of chopped logs thirty feet high. They brought the corpse from the cage and suspended it by a rope on a vertical shaft. When the flame embraced only the bark of the logs and just touched the rags of the dead man, the smoke was black and low and continually fell to the ground like trampled tufts of plume. The crowd withdrew in a semicircle to the edge of the courtyard, driven back by the first blast of heat and the pungent smoke in their eyes.

Finally the wood, too, caught fire. At once the fire fell heavily on all sides. The pink tongues of flame chased each other and joined, encircling, like a crown atop the pyre, the pole with the body hanging from it. Like a column of the whitest sheep fleece, the smoke rose higher than the gallery crowning the *Torre del Papa* and then split into hundreds of skeins that looked like petals of a withered flower. The smoke was so dense that it completely concealed the burning corpse. Scarcely two or three times could one glimpse his long body enveloped in the flames and his head pinned round with blazing feathers.

The last moments of the scorching day seemed to excite the flames of the pyre. The logs burned rapidly with a dry crackle, and had they not been laid so tightly and compactly, the burning tower would have tumbled down in a few minutes—too tall to maintain its balance very long. Instead, it turned into a solid red block, broken only here and there by fissures. The rope burned through and broke, and the corpse fell face down on the top of the pyre and soon seemed almost to melt into the embers of the topmost layer.

Had anyone tried to read in the faces of the spectators their feelings from the moment when the body of the heretic of Bolsena was dragged from the cage to the moment when it fell from the stake on the pyre and sank into the flames, he would have had before him an intricate chart of human passions. The people had wanted to tear the dead man apart and throw him to the dogs, and it had taken an iron ring of guards to keep the crowd at a distance. While the pyre was being built their hatred grew with every log that was added; had it been possible, hands driven by wrath would have raised a tower of wood that reached to the roof of heaven—so that God could better see the victim. However, no sooner did the fire slide over the surface, soar aloft, and swaddle the pyre with black shrouding, than the people fled, driven back not only by the smoke and heat but as if by the sight of their own deed. The pyre was a frail and powerless charm against the secret menace of fate that weighed on their hearts. The immolated had suddenly become very like the immolator. Whose path has the demon of despair never once crossed? Bound by the same chains to the turnspit of life, the galley slaves tortured their weaker comrade, who fell with blasphemy in his mouth and could, by his fall, hasten the *Dies Irae*. Thus has the world turned for ages, but no one knew from whose bosom would burst the next outcry of disbelief. The flames lurked at every turn, their brightness illuminating rather all of human woe than the death of one unfortunate creature. And like a final exorcism there resounded among the standing figures a choral song, that joined a plea for grace and deliverance together with a mournful dirge for the body that had been transformed into a torch.

At first they sang softly, the thin whining voices of the women sounded more clearly than the men's. The words were meaningless. They fell discordantly, striking each other or passing by in mutual pursuit. But the tone was infallible—the same notes of supplication and grief were continually repeated. From a distance one would never have guessed that the sounds of the singing were accompanied by the hiss of a hellish fire.

Only when the corpse fell on the pyre did the song change into a cry—confused and laden with threats. The crowd rolled forward as if again it would strive to break the cordon of guards, fearing neither the embers nor the raging flames. What more did they want from one who no longer existed even as a dead and mournful puppet, who before the eyes of everyone had turned into a handful of ashes?

Till late at night passersby again and again circled the cone of dying logs, which were now covered by a scale that went out and then flared up again in the darkness, hurling knife-shaped flashes at the Pope's Tower. Some people came up close and seemed to stare into the fire for the remains of the apostate of Bolsena. Nothing was left for them except an iron tear imperceptible to the eye—a small cross that had melted into a tiny ball.

At dawn the night guards rounded up a small group of beggars to clean away the ashes. Over sleeping Orvieto there soon rose what appeared to be a white cloud of snow. The dawn wind may have carried a small bit to the garden of the Palazzo Vescovile and with it dusted the eyes of the solitary old man who sat motionless on a bench beneath a tree and watched the waking of the day at the foot of the Umbrian fortress.

VI

Several days went by. At noon on Sunday a group of horsemen appeared on the road leading from the valley. They clambered up, jabbing the sweating horses with their spurs and all but sundering the horses' muzzles with the continual jerking of the bridles. The riders wore the faces of messengers bearing great tidings. Reaching the level the first horse stumbled, buckled, and though violently pulled up by its rider, fell to one side, throwing him from the saddle. The others rode on. The unhorsed rider got free of the saddle and ran as fast as he could, shouting. He was disclosing great news, but from his cry one could distinguish only two words: "miracle" and "Bolsena." The papal sentinels quickly opened the gates of the palace before the newcomers. Even after the gates had been closed again, the stifled sound of horses' hooves still filtered from the palace courtyard. Then silence, and even the unlucky rider was no longer heard, now stopped in his course and swallowed up by the crowd. All eyes turned toward the window in which, through a crack in the curtain, one might catch a fleeting glimpse of the head of Urban IV.

The messengers were taken to the audience hall. They had a long wait before the doors in the opposite wall were spread open. Urban entered dragging his feet and bearing his heavy body with difficulty. Supporting him by the elbow was Maltraga, the bishop of Orvieto.

When at last the Pope took his place on the raised platform in the corner of the hall and gave the sign that they should approach, they forgot for a moment the reverence due him. They rushed toward the throne, jostling one another and banging their metal foot-gear on the brick floor. Their words feverishly broke out like half-strangled birds. The messengers remembered themselves only at the rug before the throne, as if the suddenly cut-off echo of their own steps had reminded them on whose countenance they were about to look. They did not need Maltraga's reproving glance to bring them to their knees with hands folded over their abdomens and heads bowed on their breasts.

Urban seemed to doze as he listened to them. His lids were half closed, his hands hung limply over the armrests, and his full and slightly swollen face did not betray the slightest traces of attention. But whenever they interrupted one another or began to quarrel over details, whenever they raised their voices, again forgetting that they had been admitted to the presence of his Holy Majesty, he inadvertently tightened his fingers on the armrests and raised his lids slightly. Then his colorless eyes took on an expression of impatience, the expression of all mortally ill men whose last thoughts are already entering other zones, and who are beseeching the obtrusive world to leave off its vain noise.

"God knows that it is true," he said softly, having

heard them to the end. "I, however, His deputy on earth, forbid you to make it known."

The rider who had fallen from his horse had not yet reached the palace gate, and was finishing his account to the crowd that surrounded him in the square.

They listened to him intently and did not bother him with questions, although what he said was confused and hard to believe.

A priest, a foreigner no one had even seen before, had stopped in Bolsena on his way to Rome. At dawn he had gone to the crypt of Santa Cristina to say mass before the altar known as the *Quattro Colonne*. At first he seemed to lose his senses at the foot of the altar, and no wonder, for so recently the feet of a blasphemer had trodden these steps—a blasphemer who in the secrecy of his soul had never believed in the mystery of the Lord's Bread. Then returning to his senses, the priest went up to the altar. The mass went on slowly. There was something strange and prophetic in the atmosphere of the crypt. It was as if God were weighing whether He should make utterance with the voice of a miracle in a place where He had so long been offended. Barely three days earlier the reconsecration of the altar had been solemnly accomplished. And notwithstanding that so many dignitaries of the Church had been present and the bishop of Orvieto himself had celebrated the mass, God chose silence that time. Perhaps He wanted to reveal Himself in fingers unadorned with rings? Maybe He intentionally singled out the herald of His Second Coming in the poor and trusting pilgrim traveling from beyond the mountains and seas to His earthly capital? Suffice it to say that in the moment of the Communion the wafer of the Host was, in the fingers of the stranger, transformed into the Body of Christ and began to drip blood. The foreigner quaked, cried out, and fell senseless. They carried him to the sacristy and left him there: everyone wanted to look at the Corporal left on the altar, where the drops of blood were forming the likeness of the Crucified. The people prayed long, they raised pleas for God's grace on Bolsena, so recently stained by blasphemy, and for deliverance from plague and pestilence. When they remembered the man who had served as the blind instrument of the miracle, it was already too late. The sacristy shone empty. Runners were sent in the direction of Rome, recalling the goal of the foreign pilgrim's journey. In vain. Was he, however, only the blind instrument of the miracle? Could there have been a deeper sign in his disappearance?

"Urban! Urban!" someone called out, and others repeated the call. The name, hitherto uttered timorously and unwillingly, now fluttered around the square. Around the rider and then around those nearest him, the cries were loudest. Several women pushed back the papal sentries and approached the palace gates. A monk shouted: *Secundus Adventus!* and summoned them with a loud voice to the *Torre del Papa* to preach at the place of the holocaust that had given such wonderful fruits. Fresh riders were recruited to hunt for the stranger, and soon a large host galloped into the valley. At the crossroads at the foot of the hill of Orvieto they separated in three groups. Again and again the people called up to the curtained windows of the palace and demanded Urban.

VII

He sat immobile, his legs resting stiffly on a footstool, and stared at the large crucifix on the wall as he fingered the black beads of a rosary. It had been a long time since he had heard those voices at the foot of the palace wall. He had become reconciled to the picture of the crowd gazing toward his abode in silent reproach and expectation, reluctantly bowing to him in the squares and in the streets, as if it had taken an invisible hand to bend their stiff necks. For a long time he had thought that all that remained was for him to withdraw and trust that God would show greater favor to his successor. But although that cry of piety and faith was full of the love they had long withheld from him, it did not warm his heart. His mind, dried up from sleeplessness and barren as the nights that drained him, continually resounded to the echo of the words of the *De Miseria Humanae Conditionis*. Before his tortured eyes, fixed on the crucifix, the naked and gaunt body fastened to the cross turned red as if illuminated by the glare of a burning pyre, and now looked like the body that had been dragged by a rope from Bolsena to Orvieto, "to a cruel judgment, to a cruel punishment, to a sad spectacle." When the round beads of the rosary had reassured Urban of the paths along which God's decrees and human destinies run, his cold bloodless fingers turned stiff. "Woe unto you, woe, mournful mothers who brought into the world such unfortunate sons!" Why had his first impulse been to forbid proclaiming that holy news? He remembered only that a strange voice, albeit a voice he recognized from somewhere, had replaced his own: "God knows that it is true. I, His Deputy on earth, however, forbid you to proclaim it." And immediately after that came a second voice: "God knows that it is true?"

"Urban! Urban!" The shouts coming from the square were growing weaker. Why could he not relive

the moment that God had vouchsafed Innocent III in
the pulpit of Sant'Andrea? Why could he not be
granted the privilege of seeing the Holy Faith incar-
nated and worshipped in himself? Urban turned his
glance from the crucifix to the window and saw that
dusk had already fallen. He rose and went to the
small window niche cut out in the wall; he sank down
on the sill of the arched window and pushed aside the
edge of the curtain. Barely a handful of loiterers
remained in the square. But above the square the full
moon, the wafer of the Host, hung in the firmament.

At night Urban's short sleep finally came. One
dream picture so rapidly succeeded another that there
was no perceptible transition.

From Bolsena people were leading the foreign pilgrim in procession to him. The procession approached
Orvieto to the ringing of all the bells. Instead of going
out of the gates of the city to meet it in the gold of his
tiara and the white of his ermines, Urban sat shivering and alone in his usual place in the garden of the
Bishop's Palace. He was seen by no one. But among
the multicolored banners, the barred swords and
bristling lances, and the monstrances sparkling with
jewels, Urban saw a young man who held aloft in two
fingers of his right hand the clear, white escutcheon
of the moon. His face shone with the light of faith. A
sudden spasm of fear contorted the young man's face,
and Urban recognized the heretic of Bolsena. Everything was transformed, as things are transformed only
in sleep. The banners turned into a penitential shroud,
and the shimmer of the monstrances was extinguished.
The swords and lances turned down, and their sharp
heads and edges touched the wounded body that slowly
advanced to the rhythm of the jerking rope. The man's
raised hands were empty. Even as he dreamed, Urban

had the sensation of being asleep. Nevertheless he cried out that compassion be shown to the unfortunate man. No one heard his cry. No one except the victim. There was no fear in those eyes now, and the bloodless lips painfully whispered one phrase. Urban awoke and twice repeated the phrase aloud. And it seemed to him that in this way his clenched fist had torn away a clump of earth from that shore of darkness. The moon had already faded in the bruised sky.

In the morning Urban sent Maltraga to Bolsena.

VIII

Maltraga stayed in Bolsena three days. On the fourth day he despatched a messenger to Orvieto with the announcement that he was returning, bearing the miraculous Corporal. No one had found the Host, as no one had found the man in whose hands the Lord's blood had flowed.

Urban went out on foot to meet Maltraga. A baldaquin was borne above Urban to protect him from the August sun. After him came the bishops, then came two learned theologians, and, last, came the people. The crooked road from the city to the plain surrounding the hill looked like a swollen mountain stream. Both retinues, the one mounted and the other on foot, met on the banks of the Rivo Claro.

Maltraga dismounted from his horse and came on to the bridge, holding out the Corporal in his hand. On the other bank of the river Urban knelt. He folded his hands in prayer, bowed his head, and did not raise his eyes. He listened to the approaching steps. He did not stir even when Maltraga stood so close before him that he could have held out his hand to touch the border of the bishop's garment. In the prolonged

silence on the meadow, the water rustling below slid
over the stones as if it were a living body, gliding, like
a silver snake, its monotonous rustle violently wrested
its way through the narrow passes between the stones.
It could have gone on for ages, the world could have
stopped on that scene. For the world was nothing more
than the secret of death and immortality hanging like
a sword over the head of a man who saw all his misery
in the billows of the rushing river, in the sand running
down the hourglass.

But in the end Urban had to look up. On the white
cloth bloodstains formed a thorny crown, as clear as
if it had been painted with a brush. Below, two longer
strokes joined to form a beard. And no painter could
have rivaled the blank white space of the missing
face in the effigy of silent suffering impressed on the
scrap of linen by the affair of the unknown pilgrim.

They returned in triumph. The road was too narrow
and winding to accommodate all the people, who did
not want to lose sight of the relic of the miracle. The
green-gold valley, flooded brimful by the sun, trembled with the overflowing crowd. Urban advanced
slowly in the moving shadow of his baldaquin, staring
at the colored boxes of houses on the hill, at the
campanile, at the brick crown of the walls, at the thick
cool green of the garden behind the Palace. He could
almost see himself there, as if the dream had exchanged a reflection between two mirrors.

A pulpit was erected in the square before the Church
of Santa Maria. The people expected Urban to speak
at the end of the long procession. He stepped onto the
wooden podium. Overcome by fatigue, he rested his
elbows awhile on the edge of the pulpit, and then he
turned around several times holding up the white
cloth. After each turn he showed his face from behind

the cloth and without a word, his glance pale and contemptuous or only wearied, he looked on the thousands of faithful.

The people of Orvieto vowed to build for the Corporal a cathedral taller than the Pope's Tower. In its splendor the cathedral would tower over everything that human hands inspired by faith had ever raised. In its black and white walls of noble brick, in its columns encrusted with sculptures, in its ardent Gothic stained glass, in its rose windows, in its mosaics set with gold, in its slender spires, and in its architraves, it was to follow the plan of the heavenly harp whose strings were plucked by angels singing the *Gloria*.

The next year, after instituting the feast of Corpus Domini with the help of Thomas Aquinas, Urban died in Perugia.

IX

He died in agonies for which human hands could find no balm. Bloated, his back covered with sores from lying in bed for two months, his chest torn by cruel pains, still deprived of the blessing of sleep, no longer master of his body's faculties, endowed to his own loss with a sharpened presence of mind, although dumb and deaf, Urban awaited death with a heart so swollen with longing that his only hope was the thought that the illness would cause his heart to burst of its own accord. Urban cursed the gift of life.

But at the same time, when he would stretch out his hand as if to grasp something near the bed, he felt death prowling—a death he did not know and could not see. He immediately withdrew his hand. Stricken with fear, he shrank back, begging his assailant with rapidly trembling lips that this time he be spared. Every night it seemed that an enormous black beast would fall heavily onto his breast. Crushed, he altogether lost the power to move. Immobility gave him a foretaste of the insensibility of death, but it was a terrible immobility, because along with it life returned in all its intensity. He could not call out. In the gloom illuminated only by the wax candles of the chamber, all he could do was look for deliverance at the two monks who knelt at the sides of his bed. But they were more absorbed by the prayer for the dying than by the dying man. Was that what death was like? Was this what he was like, the deliverer who approached on soft paws in the dark—more menacing the more impatiently he was awaited, grimmer the more consciously one looked into eyes that showed no spark of pity? Was this the mystery of the threshold that the wanderer's foot trustingly approached but feared at the last minute to cross? Is this how man prepared himself to receive the fulfillment of the promise, to enter the vestibule of eternal life? Damned is the man to whom, heedless of his frailty, too much is offered.

During the day the hum of the streets of Perugia was so loud that it even penetrated ears obstructed by the wax of illness. Fantasies ever more frequently accompanied Urban's debility. He seemed to hear the *disciplinati* singing the *laudi*. When he closed his eyes, he saw their hoods and the processions slowly flowing from the hill to the valley, toward a world parched by the hot breath of Satan, lashed by the drought of death's black scourge.

Toward the end he began to lose consciousness. He lost consciousness for the first time on the day he asked for the New Testament. It was set out for him on a slanted reading stand just next to his head, which was propped on pillows. A monk turned the parchment pages. Several times the sick man signalled by lowering his eyelids. Only this mute sign suggested that he really read and did not just pass his eye over the sharp visors of the letters, ignoring the sense of the words they formed. He fell asleep at the chapter on the Crucifixion. Starting awake, he raised his impotent hand with difficulty and laid his finger on the verse: "Then Jesus, aware that everything was accomplished, in order to fulfill the Scripture, cried 'I thirst.' " Nervously, as if with a bony rod, he tapped the phrase "I thirst," so that the monk guessed his thought and brought him water. But his lips, instead of sticking to the edge of the vessel, twice repeated "I thirst," and his hand on the page of the Bible clenched into a fist, as if he were afraid to lose again that single phrase he had carried away from his dream a year earlier. His head fell to one side so suddenly that his bearded chin struck the vessel and spilled it. Only then did he really lose consciousness for the first time.

Three days he was in dying, agonizingly suspended between the dark and the brief returns of lucidity.

The fourth day at dawn they anointed his bloated and already putrefying body with holy oils.

At noon he sighed deeply, and that was his last sigh.

X

As for the unknown pilgrim, church writings tell us that his name was Peter, that he came from Prague, and that he set out on his journey to the Apostles' tombs tormented by the fear that he was losing his faith. And they tell that he disappeared without a trace, like one of those figures God brought forth from obscurity and then sent back as soon as he accomplished the purpose for which the will of Providence had called him.

But the late-thirteenth-century Czech chronicle of Bulatius records two other versions. According to one, Peter went to Rome after the miracle in Bolsena and was "consumed by such pride that he considered himself more worthy than Urban to mount the Throne of Peter." He was secretly beheaded, and his remains were cast in the Tiber. According to the second version, the monk never went to Rome at all, but set out from Bolsena to return to Prague. During his stay at a monastery outside Ferrara "he lost his senses and ended his days immured in an underground cell, because his madness manifested itself in interrupting the monks at Communion with the blasphemous cry 'Empty hands.'" He was suspected, too, of conspiring with Satan and of initiation in the Black Mass.

Plagues raged throughout the next hundred years. And every day the Second Coming was expected. Meanwhile Jews were burned, as well as heretics accused of profaning and deriding the Holy Host. In Urbino the seventeen-year-old Paolo Uccello painted some panels depicting one such episode he had heard in childhood. His *Legend of the Profaned Host* represents the story of the Jew to whom a woman sold a Host from a church. In one panel, the wafer placed on a fire gushes blood. In another, the Jew is burned, together with his wife and two children. In still another, the woman who stole the wafer is hanged. But the seventh panel of the cycle remains a mystery. This panel depicts a pair of angels contending with a pair of devils for the soul of the hanged woman.

The Second Coming was awaited, and as fervent prayers rose to heaven Jews and heretics were burned.

Jews and heretics were burned, and as fervent prayers rose to heaven the Second Coming awaited. He who was awaited came when the last embers of hope were dying. He bent over the ashes of those who had been burned alive and with His finger twice wrote a single phrase —sad and thoughtful—and then threw wide His arms as if He were once again nailed to the Cross. Legend does not record what the phrase was.

HEU, HEU, HEU,
MISERAE MATRES QUAE TAM INFELICES FILIOS GENUISTIS!

VACUE MANUS
VACUE MANUS
VACUE MANUS

LAUDATUS SIT
IN SAECULA
SAECULORUM
AMEN

FOR THE BEST IN PAPERBACKS, LOOK FOR THE 🐧

In every corner of the world, on every subject under the sun, Penguin represents quality and variety—the very best in publishing today.

For complete information about books available from Penguin—including Pelicans, Puffins, Peregrines, and Penguin Classics—and how to order them, write to us at the appropriate address below. Please note that for copyright reasons the selection of books varies from country to country.

In the United Kingdom: For a complete list of books available from Penguin in the U.K., please write to *Dept E.P., Penguin Books Ltd, Harmondsworth, Middlesex, UB7 0DA*.

In the United States: For a complete list of books available from Penguin in the U.S., please write to *Consumer Sales, Penguin USA, P.O. Box 999— Dept. 17109, Bergenfield, New Jersey 07621-0120*. Visa and MasterCard holders call 1-800-253-6476 to order all Penguin titles.

In Canada: For a complete list of books available from Penguin in Canada, please write to *Penguin Books Canada Ltd, 10 Alcorn Avenue, Suite 300, Toronto, Ontario, Canada M4V 3B2*.

In Australia: For a complete list of books available from Penguin in Australia, please write to the *Marketing Department, Penguin Books Ltd, P.O. Box 257, Ringwood, Victoria 3134*.

In New Zealand: For a complete list of books available from Penguin in New Zealand, please write to the *Marketing Department, Penguin Books (NZ) Ltd, Private Bag, Takapuna, Auckland 9*.

In India: For a complete list of books available from Penguin, please write to *Penguin Overseas Ltd, 706 Eros Apartments, 56 Nehru Place, New Delhi, 110019*.

In Holland: For a complete list of books available from Penguin in Holland, please write to *Penguin Books Nederland B.V., Postbus 195, NL-1380AD Weesp, Netherlands*.

In Germany: For a complete list of books available from Penguin, please write to *Penguin Books Ltd, Friedrichstrasse 10-12, D-6000 Frankfurt Main I, Federal Republic of Germany*.

In Spain: For a complete list of books available from Penguin in Spain, please write to *Longman, Penguin España, Calle San Nicolas 15, E-28013 Madrid, Spain*.

In Japan: For a complete list of books available from Penguin in Japan, please write to *Longman Penguin Japan Co Ltd, Yamaguchi Building, 2-12-9 Kanda Jimbocho, Chiyoda-Ku, Tokyo 101, Japan*.